MY DOM

Boston Doms - Book One

JANE HENRY
MAISY ARCHER

Published by Blushing Books
An Imprint of
ABCD Graphics and Design, Inc.
A Virginia Corporation
977 Seminole Trail #233
Charlottesville, VA 22901

Jane Henry and Maisy Archer
My Dom

eBook ISBN: 978-1-68259-565-7
Print ISBN: 978-1-64563-159-0
v1

Chapter 1

A high-pitched scream rent the unseasonably warm night air and Heidi sat bolt upright, heart pounding. Her eyes quickly scanned each corner of the still-unfamiliar bedroom for the source of the noise, but there was no movement save the soft billowing of the thin curtain in the breeze, and no sound but the soft snores of Princess, curled up at the end of the bed.

She fumbled beneath her pillow for her phone, cursing the fact that she'd yet to buy a single lamp for this place, let alone a nightstand to put it on. What moderately intelligent, thirty-year-old woman moved to a new apartment in a new city, without a lamp to turn on in the middle of the night... or to bash some-one's head with, in a pinch?

The display on the phone read 12:48. She quickly turned it to flashlight mode and swung the beam around the room. Nothing whatsoever but a tower of boxes, neatly stacked and untouched since the movers had placed them there two weeks ago. Okay. She took a deep breath as panic gave way to reason. Okay. Had it been one of the cats out in the back alley? There were plenty of them back there, though Princess strained her leash and valiantly tried to yap them out of her territory every time they went for a walk. Or maybe it had been a dream? Some weird, subconscious sign that she'd been working too hard, that the fifteen-hour days she'd been putting in, trying to get her consulting business off the ground, were catching up to her? That seemed more likely. After all, whatever it was hadn't even woken Princess. *My vicious guard dog*, she thought wryly, glancing at the sleeping ball of fur.

Step one, she thought, as she settled herself back against the pillows and tried to close her eyes, *buy new lamps. Immediately. Well, after work at least. Step two, start tackling those boxes and get settled. Maybe that would—*

Another scream echoed through the night, louder this time. Definitely not her imagination. She pushed back the covers and hurried to the window. Had one of the cats fallen into the recycling area behind the building? Should she try to help? She bit her lip in indecision and pushed the curtain aside, straining her eyes against the darkness, to see if she could get a better view of the ground below. Something was definitely moving out there— slap-thump, slap-thump, like an animal trying to get out of a—

Oh. Gah! Sweet Jesus. From across the narrow alley, Heidi could make out dim shapes moving just beyond the window. *Not a trapped animal*, she thought in disgust, letting the curtain fall again. At least not in the traditional sense. Just her neighbor, the Christian Grey-wannabe in 6F, tying it on with his girl du jour.

She blew out a breath and turned, sinking back against the wall, annoyed with herself for panicking and aggravated that she had left the window open in the first place. After all, she'd heard this little concert before.

Last Friday, when she'd first heard loud slapping followed by a woman's soft cries, she'd done what anyone would do and grabbed her phone to dial 9-1-1. And wouldn't that have been a lovely way to meet her new neighbor? She snorted. Fortunately, before she could hit *Call*, she'd heard the soft voice counting in

2

time to the slaps, and realized what she was hearing. A punishment scene, just like in one of the novels she'd read. A submissive being spanked, probably for breaking some trumped-up rule, and counting out the strokes. Totally not Heidi's thing *thankyouverymuch*, but not exactly criminal. Heidi had shut the window firmly and tried to put it out of her mind.

But she hadn't kept it out of her mind any more than she had kept the window shut. Nor had she called the maintenance guy to put in her air conditioner, or bought a white noise machine, or fallen asleep with her headphones in, all of which she had resolved to do, before dismissing each one in turn. She had reasons for those things, she reminded herself. It was too stuffy with the window closed, too soon to put in the air conditioner, too uncomfortable to sleep with headphones in.

And in the past week, it had happened twice more: different female voices responding to various murmured commands, faint slaps and cracks and curious thumps. And okay, yes, maybe she'd listened a little longer both times than was strictly polite, but only because she was trying to figure out what the heck was going on in there. For safety reasons.

And maybe she had strained her neck peering out of her living room window to watch each woman make her lonely walk of shame down the front walkway to the visitor's parking area each morning, but that was only because she wanted to make sure they were okay! Not because she had been keeping track. And *not* because she'd been mentally comparing each one—a leggy blonde and a voluptuous redhead—to her own full-figured curves and long, mouse-brown hair.

She definitely hadn't been trying to catch a glimpse of her mysterious neighbor, Mr. 6F.

She was definitely not getting vicarious thrills from his performances.

The woman across the alley let out another cry, a soprano C that left Heidi's eardrums throbbing and made Princess raise her head and glance around drowsily before flopping back on the bed. Apparently Mr. 6F was putting in a special effort tonight.

"More! Yes! Oh God! Sir, yes!" the woman's high-pitched voice squealed.

Jesus. Well, at least this one knew how to use her words. Heidi swallowed.

The rhythmic thumping ceased and a deep, cool male voice rolled through the window.

"Tammy, did I say you could speak?"

That voice, oh that voice. Dark as the night and rough as gravel, it dragged across Heidi's chest like a physical caress, leaving a trail of goose bumps on her skin. As she felt her thighs clench instinctively, she realized that she'd never really heard it before, because it wasn't the sort of voice she could ever forget. Then her mind caught up to her raging hormones and she processed the words he had spoken. Holy shit!

Did I say you could speak?

That was wrong. So, so wrong, she told herself, even as her stomach dove like a roller coaster in free-fall and her nipples hardened painfully. God, what was wrong with her?

The guy was bossing that girl around, threatening her. Maybe holding her down or even restraining her while he spanked her. Heidi should be disgusted. She *was* disgusted. Wasn't she?

She closed her eyes and tried to picture the scene.

Helpfully, the voice came out of the darkness again.

"You don't make a sound unless I command you to speak," it repeated calmly, as the roller coaster in Heidi's stomach made another loop.

"That's right, honey, you nod when you need to answer me. Very good," the voice soothed, and Heidi could actually feel the words hit her like a warm tingle, spreading down her spine from her scalp down to her back.

The sudden sharp crack made Heidi jump, her eyes flying open.

"But now, you answer me. Who sets the scene, Tammy?" the voice asked smoothly.

"You… you do, Sir!" Tammy gasped, a breathless sound of pure pleasure.

"Mmmm," the voice approved. Another sharp crack made Heidi's breath catch.

"Who decided that tonight you'd be spread out in front of me, on your knees with your ass in the air?"

Heidi grabbed the windowsill for support.

"It was you, Sir!" Tammy wailed, pleading now.

"Who decides how and when I'm going to do you, Tammy?" the voice inquired calmly.

"Oh… oh, it's you, it's you, it's you!" Tammy squealed.

"You're damn right it is," the voice agreed, and then the night fell silent but for the rhythmic thumping across the alley and Heidi's hammering pulse.

Her skin felt tight and hot, and her camisole and shorts suddenly felt restrictive and chafing. Her head lolled back against the wall, her eyes tightly shut. It was so wrong, but that was the hottest thing she'd ever heard.

But even as she fought the wave of arousal, reality intruded. She pushed herself upright and pushed a trembling hand against her stomach.

The words were hot, the voice was incredibly sexy, but the tone he had used was so cold, so distant. She realized that Tammy had essentially gone through all of that by herself—the voice might as well have belonged to a vibrator for all the emotion it displayed. So calm. Too calm. What would it be like to lose control with someone, knowing that they were so rigidly in control themselves? To put yourself completely at their mercy, knowing that they weren't getting off on the experience, on being with you, but on the power they felt from controlling you?

Heidi shuddered and, five minutes too late, shut the window. Her earlier curiosity (because it was definitely, definitely not arousal) had evaporated, leaving her feeling cold and disgusted. What had sounded exciting was actually demeaning and humiliating when it was said in such a detached, impersonal way. It confirmed what Heidi already knew: no matter how hot the fantasy might be, that kind of power imbalance only worked on the pages of a romance novel. Tomorrow, when she got her lamps at the home store, she'd check out the white noise machines. And with that comforting thought, she settled herself back into bed. Alone.

Chapter 2

Dominic stood behind the bed with his arms folded across his chest, the leather strap held firmly in his hand. He knew he was pissed off, and he was trying *not to* be pissed off, but the harder he tried not to be, the more pissed off he became. He didn't know if he was pissed off at Tammy, spread across his bed with her chest down, ass in the air, panting like a dog in heat in anticipation of the next blow of the strap, or himself, for being turned on by the strapping he'd just given her.

She was gorgeous. Or at least he was supposed to *think* that she was gorgeous. He looked with admiration at the ass he'd just striped pink, and her heaving, ample chest on the bed, her mass of thick black curls spilling on the bed around her. He'd fantasized about fisting those curls when he first met her. She was fit, everything in the right place, legs that went on forever, and shit, that girl knew how to move that body. Matteo had picked up a friend of hers, and convinced him that Tammy was the perfect submissive. She was ready for someone to master her, eager to please, and her friend, the one Matteo had spent the night with, had assured him she wasn't one that came with a lot of baggage.

She was in it for the kink, liked to be tied up and spanked, and would be eager to please in a bedroom scene.

Oh, she was absolutely in it for the kink. And God, she wanted to please, so bad it made him sick.

And that made him mad. He was mad, because he didn't know why the scene wasn't fulfilling. Wasn't *he* in it for the kink? And hell, wasn't he looking for someone who was eager to please him?

Making a show of pacing behind her, he tried to calm his anger, but she apparently took the pacing as him intentionally building up anticipation, while she squirmed eagerly. When she tilted her head to the side, he could detect the smallest glimpse of a giddy smile. He was damn glad he'd commanded her into silence, because all she did was twaddle on and on as if she'd gotten her lines from a porn flick.

"Oh, please, master," "My job is to hear and obey, sir," "Harder, please," "I want you to pound into me!" His eyes almost crossed on the last one, and he regretted the decision to not gag her. Gagging wasn't his thing, but he was beginning to see the benefits.

It was getting late. Tired, and despite his mental state, fucking turned on, he needed to bring this scene to an end before he really *did* lose his temper. He wanted release and a good night's sleep. Coming up behind her, he went through the motions. The strap fell to the floor.

"Stay on your knees," he growled, grateful she was face down and he didn't have to look at her or kiss her. She nodded into the bed, good little submissive that she was, as he took her, telling himself he was pleasing her, fulfilling a mutual base desire. And as he ground into her, he was careful not to hurt her, indulging purely in the carnal desire he had for the girl beneath him, focusing on the curve of her ass and swell of her breasts. Taking a handful of her gorgeous locks in his hand, he pulled her head back, just enough to cause her to moan but not enough to really hurt her, as he truly did want to feel that hair in his hands. He well knew this would be the last night he'd let this girl in his bed, and he might as well get in his kinks while he could.

"Please," she gasped. "Oh my God, let me come!"

Dom didn't even bother slapping her ass for talking, grateful they were almost done already.

"Yes," he spat out, and it came as no surprise that when she finally came, she screamed like a rabid animal.

"Oh my God! Oh my God, yes, yes, *yes!*" He closed his eyes tightly, focusing on something, anything, that would help put him out of his misery. The softness of the woman beneath him. The memory of the sound of the leather cracking as he swung the strap. She lay limp as he groaned, bracing himself above her, and when he was done, he rolled over onto the bed with abandon. He closed his eyes tightly so he didn't have to see her sex-sated eyes mooning at him.

Doing what any good dom would do, though it came more from trying to appease his guilt than a true concern for her welfare, he showed her where she could clean up, and tossed her a blanket so they could catch some sleep before he kicked her ass out in the morning. No cuddling. It was not uncommon for a dom to set the terms of post-sex protocol, and she could pout, but whatever; he needed some damn shuteye. It was his damn vacation, after all.

For a moment he entertained the thought that maybe he'd luck out and she'd want to hightail it home now, and he could get some sleep alone in his own bed.

No such luck.

She wanted fucking *pillow talk*.

"I swear to God, that was the best spanking I ever got, and believe me, I've gotten lots of spankings. You are *so good*. I mean, you've obviously had lots of practice. I was with this one guy who was a Dom, or at least he *called* himself a Dom. Seriously, the guy was all *slap slap slap* and I didn't even feel it, plus he didn't say a thing and just stood there like a—"

"Tammy," he interrupted, eyes shut tight, forearm slung over his face.

"Yes?" he heard her ask.

"I don't want to talk right now. Let's get some sleep."

She sighed. "I was just trying to tell you that you were really good," she said in a whiny voice that had suddenly risen several octaves. He opened his eyes. Her lower lip stuck out and his stomach twisted at the pathetic, fabricated puppy-dog eyes she was giving him. Maybe she *wasn't* eager to please. Apparently, that was just a show in bed. Figured.

"Thanks," he said with forced politeness. The quicker he pacified her, the quicker she'd go the hell to sleep and so, theoretically, would he.

"I've been with lots of other Doms," she prattled on, "and really, you are *amazing*. Like, top of the line. I think next time, I want to—"

The phrase 'next time' sent him bolt upright. He glared as she stared at his bare chest, and the definition in his abs, his sideways posture giving her a prime view. To his horror, she reached a finger out and caressed the top of his shaved head and continued to trace it down to the scruff of his beard.

"And oh my God, I swear, you look like an amped-up, sexified version of Mr. Clean or something. I've never been with a Dom with a shaved head before and I—"

"Tammy!" he spat out through gritted teeth, using what little remained of his self-control to remove her adoring fingers from his head and place them deliberately on the bed. "Mr. Clean is *bald.* I'm not bald. And I mean it."

"What?" she said, the singsong tone of her voice gone now, as her lip went out again.

"No talk. *Sleep.*"

She glared.

10

But two could play this game, and fortunately, he had the upper hand.

Narrowing his eyes, he gave her 'the look', the look he used at school to convey to his students without words that there'd be hell to pay if they didn't shape up.

She huffed.

"Lay down," he ordered in a low, stern voice. "Roll over. And go to sleep."

"I can't just go to sleep!" she protested. "Just wham, bam, go to sleep ma'am?"

Hanging onto his temper with the last shred of self-control he had, he deliberately inhaled. "Do you *really* want another spanking?" he asked.

Her eyes widened, then gleamed. "Well, I didn't know you'd be ready that soon, but if you really—"

His temper snapped.

"You say you've been with lots of Doms? Let me ask you this."

She leaned in, eyes wide but a bit apprehensive. "Um, yes. And yes?"

He lowered his voice to just above menacing. "Have any of them ever given you a *real* spanking? One that didn't end in sex? A good, hard spanking that teaches you to behave yourself and obey?"

She blinked, frowning.

"Well. No," she said.

"Do you want tonight to be the first time?" he continued in a low whisper.

"No," she whispered back.

"Then *go to sleep.*"

She frowned. "Fine," she muttered, and to his relief, she rolled over on her side, away from him, and pulled the blanket up over her shoulder. Despite her insistence that she wasn't tired, within minutes he heard light, whiffling snores. He sighed with relief and fell back on his own pillows, willing himself to sleep. He tried to relax, focusing on the soft, fluttering curtains at his window, the night air—

He sat upright.

Fluttering curtains? Night air?

He leapt out of bed.

Holy *shit!* She did *not!*

He spun on his heel and glared at the sleeping form on his bed. The only thing preventing him from waking her ass up, hauling her out of bed, and delivering that 'real' spanking he'd threatened, was the knowledge that she would be awake again, not asleep, and, therefore, delay his plan in getting her out of his house.

He'd told her very clearly to shut and lock the window, as he'd made sure his front door was locked.

She'd disobeyed him. He *knew* her friend had mentioned Tammy was a bit of an exhibitionist, but… *shit!* How had he not realized she'd left those windows open on purpose? With a stifled groan, he peeked under the curtains, as if he could tell by looking out his window if anyone had heard anything. No one was out there, of course, but with the row of windows across from him… God, if anyone he worked with ever found out—professionals at his rank did *not* pick up girls at kink clubs—and just after the scandal, too, when the board was just itching for a chance to clean up their reputation.

He sighed, as he shut the window and locked it. Nothing he could do about it now.

With a final glare at Tammy, he yanked his pillow and a blanket off the bed, and marched off to his living room to sleep on the couch.

Chapter 3

Heidi leaned her elbows on the counter, staring intently at her ancient coffeemaker as it groaned and hissed, as if her focus could encourage it to brew faster.

"Come on, baby. You can do it," she encouraged, but the machine couldn't seem to hear her over the sound of its own sputtering, and it took its sweet time, as always. She could practically hear Paul now, telling her to ditch the thing and buy herself one of those cool single-cup doohickeys, but she knew she wouldn't. Unlike her assistant, who was constantly on the hunt for the newest and the best, Heidi was a creature of habit. She'd stick with this coffee pot until it finally bit the dust. Or until she finally threw it off the fire escape in a fit of un-caffeinated rage.

With a pained sigh, she turned and slid down the cabinet to the floor, resting her forehead on her bent knees. These late nights had to stop. She'd moved to Boston to make a healthy change, personally and professionally, to increase her client base, to take on new challenges, to get out of her comfort zone… and yeah, to get just a little distance from her family who, as much as she loved them, could take her from zero to crazy in two-point-four seconds. Portland was plenty close enough to visit, but far enough away that her mother wouldn't be dropping by to inspect the contents of her refrigerator for artificial preservatives, and her incurably romantic younger sister wouldn't constantly be trying to fix her up with anything that had two legs and a penis.

Princess tiptoed over and prodded Heidi's arm with her nose in a dignified way, a queen who'd been forced to come begging. Heidi huffed in amusement and unbent to pull the little dog into her lap.

"Poor Princess," she said, gently stroking the dog's silky head and scrunched up face. "It's not easy to go from being the center of attention to the sidekick, is it, baby? You miss Mr. Reynolds, don't you?"

When her mother's elderly neighbor had fallen and broken his hip earlier this year, his family had realized, *a little too late*, in Heidi's opinion, that Mr. Reynolds couldn't live alone any longer. So, they'd moved him to an assisted living place, apparently not knowing (or not *caring*) that the place wouldn't accept his beloved dog, Princess Daphne Du Maurier (Mr. Reynolds being a big fan of *Rebecca*). Poor Princess had been left in... how did they say it in the old-school romances? *Reduced circumstances*. Heidi had been glad to take her in, but Heidi knew she was a poor substitute for Princess's real master.

"No antique carpets to piddle on in this place, huh?" she asked the dog. "No fancy dog collars. No one to cuddle with all day. But it's better than the pound, right? Better than being locked up."

Princess sank her head onto Heidi's thigh with a sigh of agreement and closed her eyes.

Heidi leaned her head back on the cabinet, patted the dog absentmindedly as she listened to the coffee maker give the loud *gurgle-hiss-splat* that she knew was the crescendo right before the end, *thank God*, and mapped out her day.

First step, coffee. Of course. Then, since Paul was celebrating his arrival in Boston by spending a long weekend on Cape Cod with some friends, there was no reason to rush to the office. Instead, she'd pull all the documentation Paul had acquired on their new client and review it. The all-important first meeting was fast approaching, and she knew from experience that she needed to be on top of her game.

She'd yet to work on a contract where the employees actually *welcomed* an outsider coming in to audit their financials, especially when the scent of corruption was in the air. Knowing that Heidi had all that sensitive information in her possession—annual salaries, executive bonuses, corporate investments, reimbursement requests for all those late-night business meetings at Hooters—made people feel vulnerable, and vulnerable people tended to behave like recalcitrant toddlers. Still, in the Difficult Client Olympics, these guys took the gold. They hadn't responded to a single one of her requests for financial or personnel information.

Shady, much?

And all the more reason to go into that meeting prepared and in control.

Plan in place, she gave the dog a final pat and stood up to get her coffee, while Princess trotted off sedately to make a grand tour of the living room.

As her back gave an uncomfortable twinge, she realized that she needed to bite the bullet and find a new gym. It had been weeks since she'd done any exercise besides scooting moving boxes from one side of the apartment to the other. Surely some place around here had decent Pilates classes. Or maybe she could *really* bust out of her comfort zone and try lifting some weights. Maybe she could even meet some new people while she was there... or not, but at least it would get Paul off her case.

She rolled her eyes as she poured a large mug of coffee.

Paul had given her a *look* when she said she hadn't had time to meet anyone in the two weeks they'd been there—a look that said he knew exactly how little effort she'd made to meet anyone except old Mrs. Brassel from the basement apartment downstairs, and that was only to apologize for Princess running across the hardwood floors at all hours of the day. She *felt* like she'd met Mr. 6F, though. She might not know how he liked his coffee, but she knew how he liked his... well.

She scraped her hair up in a ponytail and ignored the rush of heat to her face. She would not go there. Not this morning. *Or at all.* She had even carefully avoided the front window this morning, deliberately *not* sneaking a peek at the latest member of 6F's harem. It was none of her business.

But as Heidi added cream to her cup, she found herself remembering the raspy voice in the night, the desperate pleasure of the woman he'd taken so... so *forcefully*, and she shivered, just as she had a few hours ago.

Shaking her head at her wayward thoughts, she lifted the steaming mug in both hands, gratefully anticipating that first delicious sip...

When all hell broke loose.

Princess began barking... *barking*, as she hadn't barked in months, if ever, and the sound was so startling that Heidi's hand jerked, and the scalding hot coffee spilled all over her blue camisole and dribbled down her shorts. *Shit!* From the living room, Princess continued to bark wildly, and Heidi could hear the dog's claws scrabbling against the large bay window, and then across the floor to the front door. She yanked the soaking fabric of her camisole away from her reddened skin, grabbed a dishtowel from the counter, and ran to the front room.

"What is it, Princess?" she asked. "God, what happened?"

Princess was scrabbling frantically at the front door now, whining.

Oh, God! Princess hadn't been outside yet this morning, and Heidi had been too busy daydreaming about her sex-maniac neighbor to remember. *Ugh. Way to be a responsible dog owner, Heidi.*

She quickly unlocked both deadbolts and grabbed Princess's

leash ("Pink with rhinestones, as befits royalty," her sister Hillary had said when she'd given it to the dog) from the coat rack near the door, but then she paused.

She was still in her pajamas.

Her very wet, coffee-stained pajamas.

Shit.

"Okay, Princess, I need you to stay right outside this door. Do you hear me?" she told the dog sternly. Princess, who had calmed down slightly at the sight of the leash, sat on her hind legs and whined as Heidi clipped it on her collar. Was that a yes? It would have to do.

Heidi opened the door a crack, and held the leash as Princess took a cautious step onto the landing. She seemed to hesitate for a moment, walking in a slow circle, sniffing the air... then without warning, gave a mighty yelp and leaped down the stairs, pulling the leash from Heidi's unsuspecting hand, and plowed across the strip of grass in front of the building, heading straight for the street as though the hounds of hell were on her tail.

"Princess!" Heidi cried.

Her bare feet hit the landing a second later, and she pelted down the sidewalk after the wildly yapping dog.

"Stop!" came a voice so deep and stern that Heidi almost instinctively obeyed it.

Oh, *shit*. Oh *no*. The sound of Princess's excited whines was coming from...

"I said *stop*," came the voice again, and Princess's yelping immediately stopped.

Shit on a stick.

Princess had just become Mr. 6F's latest submissive.

Heidi stopped at the end of the path to the building next door. A man with close-cropped hair and bare feet was kneeling on the stoop next to her dog, one hand firmly on Princess's collar, the other patting her head in a soothing way, while Princess gazed up at him with adoring eyes. As Heidi moved to come forward, the man's eyes lifted and locked onto hers, and Heidi couldn't look away.

Green. Pale, beautiful green. Even from twenty feet away, she knew their color with certainty, and some distant part of her brain marveled. Green like jade. Green like a laser beam… like a *tractor* beam, she corrected, as she found herself walking up the path without conscious thought. And that hot, green gaze traveled the length of her, from her bare feet, up her bare legs, over the wet silk of her top, to the hair spilling out of her ponytail, and back to her eyes again. Heidi's stomach tightened in excitement. *Just from his eyes!* Imagine what it would be like if he…

Movement off to the right broke the spell, and Heidi was startled to find a woman… oh, God, *the* woman—*Tammy*—standing there watching the man and the dog, as well. Her black hair hung in limp tangles around her face, traces of old eye makeup lingered beneath her eyes, and her skin-tight dress was just a little *too* tight for broad daylight on a spring morning, but she was undeniably a knockout.

Heidi felt a blush stain her cheeks as a long strand of hair fell out of her loose ponytail to cling to her face. Could she possibly look any worse at this moment? *Doubtful.* Pale face gone red, dull blue eyes bleary from lack of sleep, half-dressed. She crossed her arms over her chest to gain some tiny semblance of modesty and felt her face grow exponentially redder. *God*, her nipples were hard! No wonder Mr. 6F was still staring.

But Tammy seemed not to notice. She was looking at the man with exactly the same expression that Princess was wearing.

Probably the same expression Heidi was wearing, too.

Mortifying.

"Oh, you are *so* brave," Tammy breathed, and the man turned away from Heidi to look at her with one eyebrow raised.

"Seriously, Dom, that thing was going to bite me."

Dom. Mr. 6F was named… no way. He was *named* Dom? His mama must've been psychic.

Heidi bit her lip as amusement cut through the mortification.

"This *thing* is a dog. And it's too small to hurt anyone... but itself," he added, with a stern look at Heidi.

The admonishment chafed more than it should have.

"She's fast," Heidi blurted, tilting her head up to look at Dom where he crouched on the top step. "She was on the front stoop and pulled away from me when I didn't expect it. I apologize. It won't happen again. I... Oh, I'm Heidi from 6E,"she said, indicating her own front door just steps away.

"Dom," the man said, confirming his name with a nod.

"And *I* was almost breakfast!" Tammy retorted, apparently feeling that no one understood the gravity of the situation. "That thing is small but vicious. He jumped on me and practically knocked me down! If I get knocked down again, I... I'll *sue.*"

It was Heidi's turn to raise an eyebrow.

"Princess is a *she*," Heidi said hotly, grabbing Princess's trailing leash with a pointed look at the pink and rhinestones. "She *never* bites. And I have *never* known her to jump on anyone... but frankly, I've never known her to get so excited or to run away, either," she admitted.

Tammy sniffed derisively, and Heidi's temper flared.

"I'd hate to think you *smacked yourself* on anything or got *hurt* in any way. Maybe we should take you to the doctor? See if you got *bruised?*"

Tammy's eyes flicked to Dom for a moment, then she stood up straighter.

"No, that won't be necessary," she said stiffly.

"No, in fact, you were just leaving, weren't you, honey?" Dom said, straightening from his crouch. His tone left no room for argument.

"I-I do have to get going," Tammy said with dignity, but her eyes were still trained on Dom, as though hoping he would relent.

He didn't.

Tammy hitched her purse under her arm and stalked down the steps, not bothering to acknowledge Heidi.

"Nice meeting you!" Heidi called with a mocking wave. "You have a great day, too!"

She turned back to Dom, and could swear she saw his lips twitch.

"So, sorry again about this," she said, lifting her hands to indicate the dog, Tammy, and herself. "I'll just take Prin..."

"You know, we have rules in this complex," he said, folding his arms across his chest and walking... *stalking*... slowly down the stairs. "Rules about *dogs*," he elaborated. "And leashes."

Heidi flushed.

"Those rules protect everyone's safety," he concluded when he was standing right in front of her.

"I know... I just... It was kind of an emergency," she stammered. "And I was holding the leash. I didn't expect her to pull away like that."

"Sounds to me like you need a firmer hand on the leash."

He did not just say that to me.

Heidi looked up at him, eyes widening in amazement at the double meaning, but his return look was bland. God, she was paranoid.

She cleared her throat.

"It won't happen again," she promised.

"See that it doesn't," he said softly but sternly, sending an uncontrollable flush of warmth through her body and making her fucking traitorous nipples harden again, right there on the spot.

Quickly folding her arms across her chest once more, a quick glance at his face told her he suspected exactly what she was trying to hide.

Some demon compelled her to add, "I'm really sorry about Tammy. She seemed fairly traumatized."

He smiled, a smug, knowing glance that should have warned her, but didn't.

"I wasn't aware that you two were on a first-name basis," he drawled.

Tammy hadn't given her name. Caught.

Heidi could feel her face flush.

"Well, trauma brings people together quickly," she joked in a strangled voice, pretending to misunderstand.

He merely nodded, but she had the sense that he was fighting off laughter.

"Right," she squeaked. "Well. Nice to meet you. Come on, Princess."

Heidi walked quickly down the sidewalk, but the blasted dog refused to go.

"Princess! Come!" Heidi said sternly.

But the dog gazed forlornly at Dom, and refused to be budged.

She inhaled sharply. Honest to God, if she had to bend down in this outfit to pick up her dog, that would be the final...

But she didn't even have time to complete the thought, because Dom knelt down, caught Princess's eye, rubbed her head, pointed firmly at Heidi's door, and sent the dog running back home, eager to do his bidding, trailing a mortified Heidi behind her.

Chapter 4

"**D**on't move until I tell you. Keep your hands right there and do what I say."

Dominic lay on the weight lifting bench, pursing his lips with a glare at his wiseass brother.

"I'm not your fucking sub, Matteo," he growled.

His twin brother, a mere four minutes his junior, stood over him and glared back. Dom looked up at a near mirror image of his own reflection, the same short-cropped hair and green eyes. A tattoo of a skull and crossbones, with the words *Death before Dishonor,* flanked the uppermost part of his right arm.

"You're on the bench and I'm spotting you; you're my fucking sub," Matteo said out loud, with a good-natured grin. "You wanna break your neck or knock your teeth out, do it on your own time."

Dom snorted, though his laughter immediately fled as he lifted the bar up. Matteo wasn't fooling around. He really had upped the chest weight. Dom pushed, every muscle and tendon straining and flexing, while Matteo stood over him, braced and ready.

"Push for muscle fatigue," Matteo always said, mixing up shit concoctions in his blender for Dom before and after they hit the weights. "You wanna break 'em down then build 'em back up again."

Matteo had learned a shitload of bodybuilding protocol in his stint overseas, and he helped Dom train as well. At first, Dom was reluctant, but he soon came to enjoy the high after a hard workout, the challenge of the bench, and most of all, the effects of his workouts. He never would push to be a large, Hulkish bodybuilder, but there were decided benefits in strength training.

Matteo had always been first at everything. When they were kids, he was the first to hit the playground. First one to win a race. First to decide what he was doing when they graduated high school. First to learn how to weight train.

First to take a submissive.

Never one to hide what he did, he was open and honest with Dom and their brother Tony about how he liked things. It was only a matter of time before Dom was curious himself, and his hangups about telling a girl what to do, or inflicting measured pain, fled when he realized how erotic the whole scene was when cloaked in the consent he was always careful he had in place. Matteo did things boldly, with abandon and no apology. So, after polishing off a six-pack to whet their whistles one night when Matteo had returned home, he'd hooked Dom into coming, and taken him into a fairly tame club near Kenmore Square.

A whole new world was opened up to Dom.

That had been ten years ago. Unlike Matteo, Dom had eased into things, trying out what he liked and didn't, making careful choices as to whom he brought home.

Dom was always, always careful to be sure the girls he took home weren't looking for full-time. Matteo had warned him in the beginning—full-time, long-term was serious shit. In it for the kink, there were plenty of options, but if he didn't wanna be some girl's daddy, he had to choose carefully.

It pleased Dom to know that his naturally stern, take-charge demeanor and desire for control were, contrary to what he'd believed to be true, actually *attractive* to a certain type of girl. And it pleased him to know how erotic the shit could be.

"Good," Matteo said, lifting the bar and replacing it on the rack. "Time for some lower body shredding. Get up."

"No."

Matteo's eyebrows shot up. Dom chuckled.

"Get over yourself, Matt," he said, getting to his feet and on the mat, grabbing the bar to start their squats. He liked pushing his brother's buttons. As close as two siblings could be, they rarely actually got into a fight. Still, one dominant personality versus another, egos occasionally battled it out, though they mostly understood each other. If push came to shove, they had each other's backs. What happened at a club stayed at a club. Though everything they partook in was consensual, they knew the dangers a dominant faced. Secrecy and caution prevailed.

"Shit," Matteo muttered under his breath. "Why don't these assholes do some real training here? They've at least gotta hire some floor monitors that know their asses from their elbows. Somebody's gonna kill themselves one day." His eyes were focused on a workout station behind Dom, and he was shaking his head as if disgusted. Dom casually craned his neck to see what Matteo was griping about, and when he did, he almost dropped the bar.

It was her. That sexy-as-all-hell girl from the day before, apartment... what did she say again? 9A? 8G? Whatever. Had she told him her name? Pollyanna or something? He remembered her yippy dog. Forget about the girl's steel blue eyes and those high cheekbones sprinkled with adorable freckles. Her full, wavy, chestnut-colored hair she'd been wearing in a messy up-do thing, had barely covered her voluptuous full figure with the skimpy outfit she'd been wearing. And now was no different. He'd given thanks to the gym gods many times for the way women's gym clothes were designed. The girl was wearing a vibrant blue top, and black capris, the stretchy material of the workout pants making her ass look delectably spankable.

"She's gonna break her neck," Matteo muttered, and as Dom looked, he could tell Matteo was right. She'd probably looked up some workouts on YouTube or something, as the girl clearly hadn't had any training, tipping sideways in a move that looked vaguely like a lunge.

"I know that girl," Dom said in a low voice, turning his back to her again and facing Matteo.

"Girl? She's no girl. She's a full-blown woman," Matteo corrected.

"No shit," Dom said in a strangled voice.

"How do you know her?" Matteo lifted the bar up and over his head, laid it on the meaty portion of his back, and started squatting, his eyes still trained behind Dom.

"Apartment near me," Dom panted, suddenly short on breath as he followed Matteo's squat position. Shit, that hurt.

Matteo grunted in return.

"Think she's into the scene?" Matteo asked, as he stood again.

Dom grunted. He remembered the way she mentioned Tammy's name. Clearly, she'd been privy to *something*. He'd seen the way her cheeks flushed and eyes widened when he'd intentionally, nonchalantly dropped the line about a firmer hand on the leash. Was she into the scene? Maybe not. Could she learn to like the scene?

Hell yeah.

"No."

Matteo frowned. "Too bad," he said, his eyes still trained on her. "Hey, I saw your Tammy at The Club last night. You let her flirt with other men?"

"She can flirt with whomever the hell she wants to flirt with. And she's not 'my' Tammy."

"Shit, man, I wish I knew that last night."

Dom squatted down, exhaling as he came to his feet.

"You're better off staying away."

"Yeah? She's shit in bed? Tries to top from the bottom or something?"

"Clingy, manipulative, sent me twenty-seven texts after I told her we were done. And by all intents and purposes, I made it clear it was a one-night thing we were into, no more."

Matteo whistled low. "You had me at clingy."

Dom snorted. He strategically moved so he could get a better view of the girl. Had she noticed them? He watched. She'd replaced the barbell she was lifting and sat down on the ab machine. There was a padded seat, weights one could adjust with a small metal lever, and once in position, the user sat up, pulling the upper pads down to squeeze the abs. She gave a slight toss of her head—Intentionally?—lifting the small lever to adjust the weight, and pushed it in. Dom's eyes narrowed. That was a fucking heavy weight she was lifting for a girl her size.

She squinted her eyes at the instructions plastered on the side of the machine.

He wanted to drop his weights and go over. What kind of an idiot figured out how to use a machine by reading the instructions on the side? She needed a real trainer. But no, it wasn't his job. She had to figure this out on her own. He did another low squat as he watched her.

She swallowed, giving a toss of her head and her eyes cut over to them. When she saw they were both facing her, she flushed.

Yeah, she'd seen them.

She dropped her head back, got into position, and tried to sit up, pulling the weights with her in a crunch. Dom bit his lip to keep from laughing. The weights didn't budge, as her face grew red and the veins bulged on her neck.

Drop the weight, girl.

Frowning, she sat up, and threw the lever down a few notches to a more manageable weight.

Good girl.

Where the hell did that come from? He felt himself oddly pleased that she'd stopped endangering herself, and was being more sensible about what she could handle. She sat back down, and crunched her way through, looking like she was gonna pass out any minute.

"Ten more reps," Matteo grunted.

Dom pushed to his feet, squatted back down, feeling the burn along his thighs and hamstrings, the weight of the bar on his back bearing down on him. He squatted low, then pushed to his feet firmly, looking away from her. He didn't need to look at her. He didn't need to see the way her skin glistened, her hair clinging to her cheeks in damp tendrils, the way her chest was heaving and her breath coming in shallow gasps. It reminded him too much of—

"Two," Matteo said, as Dom willed himself out of his sordid reverie. "One."

Dom lifted the bar over his head carefully, flipped it over and replaced the weights. Matteo stood next to him, standing on one foot, releasing his muscles, and Dom imitated his brother.

"God," Matteo said. "She's gonna kill herself."

Dom intentionally didn't spin around to look, but turned carefully. Her back was to them now. She'd grabbed her bar again, and she had a crazy weight on it. Why was she choosing such high weights? Didn't she have *any* training? Most women who trained used frequent, low reps to tone. It was the heavier, shorter reps that built muscle, and most women preferred not to bulk out. She was back in the lunge position, or what he assumed was supposed to be the lunge position. Lunges were supposed to be performed as if the feet were on railroad tracks, slow, deliberate dips of the knee, with the feet about two feet apart. One of her legs stuck out at an odd angle, but she looked determined, lips set in a straight line.

She *was* gonna hurt herself.

As she dipped low to the ground, he cringed. Her lower back was way out of line, leaning too forward, and the weight was too much for her. She wobbled as she began to dip.

Finally, her bravado failed her. She was so low to the ground that her knee was almost touching. And then it *did* touch.

Dom waited to see her get to her feet. But she didn't.

It took him about two seconds later than it did Matteo to realize she didn't get up because she *couldn't*.

Matteo was already over there.

Asshole.

Dom could tell from where he was that Matteo was in full-on pick-up mode.

The hell he was.

Dom didn't even know why he was already on his way over. Why he felt like socking his brother in the jaw. Why he felt anger surge through him when Matteo's hands grasped the bar on her shoulders and lifted the weight off of her. Why it took all he could do not to shove him out of the way when he heard his brother's low, suave voice asking her if she was okay.

But physical limitations were on his side.

Matteo had the bar in his hands as the girl tried to stand, painfully, looking as if she'd pulled something. Matteo couldn't help her to her feet.

Dom reached a hand out to her. She blinked, ignoring his hand and trying to struggle to her feet, but she nearly toppled over. He reached out and grasped her reluctant hand.

He was unprepared for how it would feel. His *plan* was to haul her to her feet before Matteo had finished replacing the bar and could get his hands on her. He didn't know when he took her small, fragile hand in his, as he towered over her, that she would wobble and trip, and that he'd have to brace her fall by placing his hand on her waist to steady her. How could he know that she would involuntarily reach out for him with a pained yelp? He didn't know that a girl who was sweaty and panting could smell so good as he placed both of his large hands on her waist, or that her wide eyes would be so transparent and heated, as they stood suddenly far too close for two people who hardly knew each other.

He felt the vibrating heat between them, an electric pulse he hadn't experienced with girls he'd taken to bed, much less with a girl he hardly knew who was standing next to him in a crowded gym. Her top was so thin, one of those flimsy wicking workout tops, it almost felt as if his hands touched the warm, soft skin beneath the top. He could feel her intake of breath, and her ragged exhale pulsed straight to his lower abdomen.

Shit.

She tried to let go, but nearly stumbled again.

He held fast.

"I… I'm okay," she said. "Gosh, thank you, I'm such an idiot, I didn't know—" Her eyes widened, as if in sudden recognition. She stood straighter, composing herself, as she continued. "It would feel so heavy when I lunged."

"Honey, that was no lunge you were doing," Dom said, and her eyes immediately flashed at him.

"Oh yeah?" she said, trying to pull away again, and stumbling. She was hurt.

Matteo stood behind her, giving him a 'what the fuck?' look. Dom gave him a 'go the hell away' look in return. Matteo sighed defeat, and stood behind them, arms crossed on his chest.

Finder's keepers.

"If you were doing a proper lunge, you wouldn't be so hurt right now."

"Oh yeah?" she said again, her voice rising.

Why was she getting so pissed off?

"Yeah," he said forcefully, feeling his own temper rising.

Why was *he* getting so pissed off?

She looked as if she were about to say something else, and she tried to pull away from him, but as she moved, she winced. It was her back. She reached for it, obviously in enough pain that it was difficult to walk. His anger softened.

"You hurt yourself," he said.

"No shit, Sherlock," she quipped, eyes squeezed shut in pain. Matteo masked a chuckle with a cough.

She had a temper, and a wiseass mouth.

Who was he to think this girl would be into the scene? She was no more submissive than he was.

"Well, maybe you shouldn't have taken so much weight on your bar," he scolded. She could mouth off all she wanted, but he was still holding her upright.

"I didn't know how heavy it would be," she said, her voice dropping as her pained eyes opened. His anger vanished.

Of course she hadn't. It was a complete accident, and he was being an asshole lecturing her on gym safety when she could barely stand.

"You're the girl I met the other day," he said. "Right? With the dog?"

She nodded. He surmised she was in too much pain to talk. She swallowed, as if trying to stop herself from crying. Shit.

"We live in the same apartment complex," he said. "I'll drive you home."

She shook her head and pulled away from him. "I'm fine to drive," she said, as she nearly toppled over and barely caught herself on a machine next to her.

"You're not fine to drive," Matteo said, as he came to her side. He was no longer scoping her out, but looking at her with concern. As he looked over his head at Dom, Dom knew. Matteo was no longer hitting on her, but had given up the fight. Now he was helping Dom.

"You got someone who can come get you?" Dom asked her.

She looked at the ground and shook her head. "Could call my assistant but he's already at the office," she said with a sigh.

"I'll drive you," Dom insisted. "But look, I've gotta head home and shower first. You've got your cell phone with you?" She nodded.

"Then let's go. You've got stuff in your locker?"

She shook her head. "I left my wallet and bag in my car."

Seriously?

"You can't leave your shit in your car!" he growled. She glared again. Matteo shook his head and raised his eyes heavenward.

"Well I did," she spat out, but her voice caught at the end. He sighed.

"All right. I'll bring you to my car, then we'll drive to yours to get your stuff." She nodded.

He fought the desire to pick her up, swing her right up in his arms and carry her to the car, stop that pained look in her eyes when she tried to move. But no. He had to ease her fear by staying calm and normal and natural.

Where had the desire to protect her come from? He hardly knew her.

Damn his dom instincts.

Matteo stood in front of her. "Matteo," he said, reaching his hand out to her. She shook it quickly, then moved her hand back to brace her back.

"Heidi," she said, looking from one to the other as if she just noticed the resemblance.

That's right. Heidi.

"And you know my brother Dom?" Matteo said. "He's a good guy. He won't hurt you. And the apartment building is like, what, two minutes away?"

Heidi nodded.

Matteo continued. "Text your assistant. Tell him Dom from your gym is driving you back to your apartment."

Good man, Matteo.

Dom would buy the next round of drinks.

"Fine," she sighed. He could tell she was reluctant to agree to this, but she really had little choice.

Dom would do his best to make sure he put her at ease. He'd be professional, and aloof, and not try to hit on her. Forget the fact that she was clinging to him and so close, her breath brushed his arm. Forget about the fact that the soft pitch of her voice went right through him, and he felt the pulse of her femininity with every breath she took and released.

She was probably overwhelmed. Sometimes it was hard to think clearly through pain. But he knew from his years as a dominant, that many women would respond well to a calm instruction, especially in a difficult situation. A simple directive would make it easier for her.

It would also be telling.

"Follow me," he ordered low.

"Okay," she whispered, with a droop of her shoulders, and he felt the tension go out of her as she clung to him.

Chapter 5

Heidi shook another dose of Tylenol into her palm and bit back a moan when even that slight motion caused her muscles to seize. The aching in her lower back was unrelenting, and it seemed to be getting worse.

Well, maybe you should stick to your regular exercise routine, and not attempt to burn off your frustrations by pushing yourself way beyond your limits, hmmm? The voice in her head was suddenly a deep, sexy, *bossy* baritone that brooked no argument.

And maybe you *should shut the hell up and get out of my head,* she told the voice, as she grabbed the magical pills and downed them with a swallow of nearly cold coffee from the mug on her desk. Honestly, of all the gyms in all the world, why had she chosen to humiliate herself in *that* one?

"Hey, didn't you already take two of those? Those pills aren't candy, you know," said another deep voice laced with disapproval.

Heidi turned her head (oh, the agony!) to see Paul, framed in the open doorway from the reception area to her office. He looked runway-ready, as always, with his artfully tousled brown hair, an immaculate, tight-fitting lilac button-down stretched across his chest, and perfectly pressed grey slacks hanging just so from his lean hips. *Sex on two legs*, Heidi thought sourly, despite the almost comical way his arms were crossed and his lips were pursed. She glanced down at her own rumpled wrap dress and flip flops—the only clothing she'd been able to get into without destroying her back, and even that only after an extremely long, hot shower—and her temper flared.

Was there some sign on her forehead today saying 'Incompetent Female! Please Boss Me Around'?

"Yes, I'm perfectly aware of that, Paul, thank you. I took a dose at nine o'clock, and the dosage instructions, created by *actual medical professionals*, say that it's okay to take two every four hours. Since it's now…" She paused to glance down at the watch on her wrist, moving her head as little as possible. "One-oh-*four* PM, I'm actually a little *behind* schedule. *Okay?*"

Paul's eyes widened in indignation and he held up his hands in mock-surrender.

"Yeah, *whatever*. God forbid someone try to help you out," he snapped. He turned and began to tidy the pile of folders atop the file cabinet which, along with her desk, two folding chairs, and the cluttered wooden table that used to live in Heidi's Portland kitchen, comprised all the furniture in her new office.

Heidi sighed. It wasn't Paul's fault she'd already reached her capacity for know-it-all men before she got to the office this morning.

"I'm sorry, Paul. Would you sit down?" she said in a resigned voice. "Please," she added, when he turned to look at her, her eyes flicking to one of the folding chairs in front of her desk.

He complied, slowly, but focused his eyes on the corner of the office behind her head, clearly not planning to make this easy for her.

"I'm sorry," she repeated. And she was, sincerely. "I *do* appreciate your concern. I'm just…" Pissed off? Exhausted? Sexually frustrated? All of the above? She sighed. "Really tired. And my back hurts."

Paul met her eyes, and his clear, blue eyes instantly lit with sympathy… and curiosity. He leaned forward.

"Yeah, how did that even happen? You go to the gym all the damn time! You're, like, the fucking *queen* of Pilates. Then I suddenly get this cryptic text saying, 'Hurt my back. Dom from the gym is taking me home.' Which, of course, makes me think you've finally landed yourself a new man, and you're taking him home for some *somethin-somethin.*"

Despite the lingering pain, Heidi snorted.

"Okay, forget *Dom,*" she spat his name like a dirty word. "Let's talk about the real story here… You get a text saying I'm injured at the gym, and your first thought is 'That must be *code* for luring a *guy* to her apartment for *sex*!' Just so I know, what would your first thought be if I texted 'Building on fire!'?"

She lowered her voice to a fair impression of Paul's deeper tone.

"Hey, this must mean Heidi's tied up in some dude's bondage playroom!"

Paul rolled his eyes to the ceiling and sat back in his chair.

She clasped her hands in front of her chest dramatically and intoned, "My darling Paul, I'm clinging to edge of a cliff. Remember me fondly."

"Well, golly gee!" she mocked in her deep Paul-voice. "Heidi must mean she's having an orgy with three fat men and an orangutan!"

"Are you done?" Paul asked severely, though his mouth twitched in reluctant amusement.

Heidi nodded magnanimously.

"Okay, first of all, I have never said 'Golly gee!' in my life," he argued with mock-dignity, as Heidi burst into laughter.

"But," he continued sternly, after she had composed herself. "Is it so wrong to hope that my best friend is finally going to lose her self-imposed secondary-virginity? It's been way too long, Heids! What happened to 'new city, new rules'? I thought the plan was to finally break out, live a little, achieve that work-life-balance thing, without your mom giving you shit every time you turn around. It's been three weeks since we officially moved here," he said, his eyes boring into hers. "How many of those evenings have you *not* spent holed up in your apartment or here at the office?"

She opened her mouth, then closed it again.

"Exactly," Paul said with a nod. "So, yeah, maybe I got a little excited to think you were out meeting a guy, instead of hiding away in here."

"I do not *hide* in here!" she protested, averting her gaze from the concern she read in his eyes. "I'm *working*, Paul! Trying to get *Heidi Morrow Consulting* off the ground requires all of my time and attention. Which you should support one hundred percent," she added wryly. "Since that will make it possible for you to actually *afford* your new fourth-floor walk-up on Union Park."

He grimaced.

"Besides which," she continued, hating the note of defensive-ness in her own voice. "It's not easy to meet new people."

He made a sound of protest, but she rolled right over him with a wave of her hand.

"Yes, yes, *you* met a couple of guys at brunch and already spent a weekend with them in P-town, and you've hooked up with however-many hot guys already this week. That's one of the things I love about you, Paul. You're freakishly good at meeting people and putting them at ease. It makes you such an asset, as an employee and as a friend. But… that's not me. So, right now I'm focusing on what I'm good at. I'm building a company."

He huffed out a breath of frustrated disagreement.

"Heidi, honey, the company is already built. You moved to Boston with enough clients already lined up to keep you busy for *years*," he began, just as the phone rang in the lobby. He stood and walked toward the door.

"You're making excuses," he accused, pointing one well-manicured finger at her as he left the room.

She sighed and stretched her back experimentally, pleased that it was finally loosening up slightly.

Was she making excuses, hiding behind work? It was true that things had been going well—even better than she'd anticipated. All of her financial goals were on track, and... Her eyes drifted to the enormous basket of gourmet chocolates that had arrived the day before, a thank-you gift from her last satisfied client... She was building a reputation for herself as a problem-solver; a knowledgeable, unbiased adviser who could walk into a company and quickly identify the weaknesses, the areas of potential waste, and help them maximize their resources, as well as their profits. Still, she couldn't afford to rest on her laurels. Her success in this arena was all about her reputation, and she had to stay vigilant to maintain it.

So, yeah, maybe she'd been working too hard. Maybe things had gotten a bit unbalanced for her. Heck, hadn't she already acknowledged that to herself just the other night? She just needed to find a hobby, a way to unwind...

Her mind immediately flew back to *that* night, to the open window and the keening cries of a woman finding her pleasure...

She ruthlessly wrenched her mind away. No. That wasn't a hobby, it was—it was—it was *wrong.* She was an independent entrepreneur, a *boss,* a *leader.* She wouldn't be a sex toy for some misogynistic *Neanderthal.* She'd leave that to Tammy and the rest of 6F's harem.

With a firm nod, she turned to her laptop and began sorting through her seventy-four unread messages.

Paul reappeared in the doorway a moment later carrying a FedEx envelope and a fresh mug of coffee. Heidi's eyes rounded.

"Is that for me?" she asked hopefully, eyeing the coffee.

"Could be," he allowed. "And this package of quarterly financials from Easterbrook Academy could be for you, too," he taunted, dangling the opened envelope in front of her face.

"No way! They finally got their heads out of their asses after three requests? Are the personnel files in there, too? Give it!" she demanded, when he continued to hold it just out of reach.

She made a grab for the package that had her back screaming in pain.

"Oh, shit," she moaned, collapsing back into her chair.

"Tsk, tsk, tsk," Paul chided. "Patience is a virtue, Heids."

She glared at him as she massaged her throbbing back.

"No, they haven't sent any personnel files yet. Just this package of thick, juicy, no-doubt-*incriminating* financials," he informed her, re-taking his seat. "But if you want it, you're going to have to earn it. Now, *what* were we discussing?"

"You're a sick puppy, you know that?" she groused.

"Yep. I've heard that one before," he said, a strange note in his voice that said he was only partly teasing.

Heidi frowned, but before she could ask him about it, Paul cut her off.

"Here," he said, setting the steaming coffee in front of her. "Now tell me a story about... let's see... *Dom*," he said, mimicking the disgusted way she'd said his name earlier.

Heidi rolled her eyes.

"I already told you, there's nothing to tell," she said dismissively, focusing her attention on the fresh mug of coffee.

"Aw, that's too bad!" Paul said cheerfully, pretending to rise from the chair. "Looks like I need to go visit *the paper shredder!*"

"Honestly," she said, smiling even as she shook her head at his empty threat. "How old are you?"

Paul grinned and clasped the envelope in front of his chest like a shield. "Older than you, chickie, though I don't look a day over twenty-five! Now *spill.*"

"Fine. *God!* Just let me get on with my day!" she said, throwing up her hands in exasperation.

"Dom is my neighbor," she recited. "He and his brother happened to be at the gym this morning at the same time I was. I was feeling guilty that I haven't been to the gym as much since we moved, and my ass is fat enough already, so I tried to up my workout routine by adding some lunges and weights. I pulled a muscle in my back and Dom's brother helped me out. And then Dom, who's a jerk, got into some kind of pissing contest with his brother and insisted on taking me home. So he did. The end."

She held out her hand expectantly for the envelope.

Paul ignored her, his brow creased in thought.

"Okay, wait. Dom is your neighbor?"

"Yeah," she said impatiently. "He lives next door, just across the alley from me. Unit 6F."

Paul seized on this detail.

"So, you already knew him before today?"

Heidi could feel the blush climbing from her chest to her face.

"I… *sorta* knew him. We're neighbors."

But Paul had obviously seen the blush and wouldn't be put off. He leaned forward, like Perry Mason out to prove his case, and simply raised one eyebrow.

Heidi squirmed.

"I… okay, *fine*, this is so embarrassing… I heard him having sex," she admitted.

Paul's jaw dropped. "You *what?*"

"He obviously likes to have the windows open and I heard him… *doing* women."

"*Women?* As in more than one?"

Heidi nodded.

"Four," she supplied.

"Four women at once?" Paul looked reluctantly impressed.

Heidi pulled a face. "No! *God*, Paul! Okay, *first*, you're a little too interested in this. This guy doesn't play for your team."

Paul acknowledged this with a shrug.

"And second… *no*, four women in the past three weeks. Individually," she felt her face grow even hotter. "As far as I know. Although with him, who knows?"

"And what does *that* mean?" Paul wanted to know.

"Just… he has… he does… *unusual things* to them."

Paul's head reared back in surprise, and Heidi was compelled to explain.

"God, not like whatever you're thinking! Not…" She took a deep breath and looked away from Paul. "He's a dominant, and he gets… rough with them. Consensually."

Paul was quiet for a moment. Then two. Heidi finally glanced up at him to see that a frown was back on his face.

"And you find that… disturbing?" he asked, his tone serious.

Heidi took a deep breath and considered the question.

"I… No. I find it… interesting, I guess. Intriguing… But purely in a fantasy-way!" she added, seeing Paul's curious expression. "I could never actually *do* that, you know?"

Paul nodded slowly, seeming to consider something, but then he continued.

"Okay… so he's a dominant. Wait, *Dom the dominant?*" he chortled, making the connection for the first time.

Heidi giggled.

"I know! I thought that, too. His mama was psychic."

"Okay, fine," Paul said, rocking his chair back with a smile on his face. "So he's a neighbor with an intriguing sex life. Hot?"

A vision of Dom, muscles on display and sweaty from his workout, appeared unbidden in her mind. She licked her lips unconsciously and nodded.

"So, you have a *hot*, intriguing neighbor who rescued you when you hurt yourself. And that makes him a jerk because…"

"He dominated my dog."

Paul's chair flew backward before he managed to right himself and bring the front legs down with a crash.

Heidi giggled again, then told him the tale of Tammy and Princess.

"Pretty sure he caught the fact that I knew Tammy's name," she concluded. "But if he didn't want people to hear, he shouldn't have opened his window, right? Anyway, he insinuated that I wasn't a responsible dog owner, while I was standing there half-naked and covered in coffee! That's not exactly chivalrous," she said.

Paul hmmed in sympathy and rubbed his chin, deep in thought.

"And then," she continued, warming to her story and glad to vent now that she had begun. "This morning after the gym thing, he helps me into his car and drives me over to my car to collect my wallet and house keys and stuff, right?"

"You left your wallet and keys in your car?" Paul interrupted.

"Yes, *whatever*. I do it all the time and I've never had a problem with it before."

"Maybe because you lived in an exclusive suburb of Portland with only 5000 residents? You're not in Kansas any more, Toto!"

Heidi sighed.

"Okay, fine. I get that. But the point of my story is that I have *already* heard this lecture, all the way across the parking lot and then halfway to my house!"

Paul nodded once, as though satisfied.

"Are you for real?" she asked him indignantly. "You're supposed to be on my side!"

"I *am* on your side, *for real*," he said calmly. "It was stupid. Now you know it. Continue," he said, waving a hand.

Heidi tamped down her flare of annoyance at the high-handedness of men.

"So, he spent the rest of the car ride lecturing me on not overdoing things at the gym," she continued. "Said I need to find

41

a better gym with a personal trainer to show me proper form and whatever."

Paul opened his mouth, but she cut him off with a sigh.

"Yes, yes, I *know*, he's probably right. The *point* is that I'm sitting there, in pain, and this guy who's practically a stranger is lecturing me. It was… humiliating," she admitted in a small voice.

Paul inhaled deeply.

"I'm sorry, sweetie. That sucks," he agreed, and Heidi found her eyes filling with tears. She nodded.

"But… honestly, I don't think he was being a jerk. He was being protective. That's what a dominant does."

Heidi snorted in disbelief.

"I've read the books, Paul. And I've heard the audio, first-hand. That's *not* what a dominant does. A dominant is all 'I made up a rule and you broke it, and now you must be punished'!" she concluded, affecting a deep, menacing voice.

Paul pressed his lips together as though fighting laughter.

"Okay," he allowed. "A dominant is *sometimes* like that, for fun or when the situation calls for it. But in general…"

His blue eyes were serious as they held hers.

"In general, a dominant is all about protecting what's *his*. And the rules he puts in place aren't arbitrary or based on his whim… *in general*," he reiterated, seeing that Heidi was about to protest. "Yeah, it sounds like this guy could've expressed himself better, since you hardly know him, but… it sounds like he was trying to be protective."

Heidi sipped her coffee. She remembered the way Dom's hand had felt, wrapped tenderly but firmly around her waist, how gentle he'd been when he'd grabbed her seat belt and buckled her in, how he'd all but carried her to her front door and offered to get her an ice pack from his own freezer, how he'd given her his cell number and told her to text him when she was ready to pick up her car. That part had felt nice, so nice. But…

"Okay, fine. So doms aren't necessarily jerks. But I'm *not* his," she said slowly, putting the mug on her desk. "And I'm not a submissive. You know me, Paul! I'm not *weak*. I have a career. I have *goals*." She gestured around the office. "I could never just sit back and let someone call all the shots."

"Doms aren't jerks," he agreed. "And, sweetie, subs aren't weaklings."

She raised an eyebrow skeptically.

"It takes so much strength to yield yourself to someone completely… such an indomitable sense of self to let someone else call the shots," he said rapturously, excitedly. "To know that someone's given themselves to you that way…"

Heidi sucked in a breath as light finally dawned.

"You know an awful lot about this," she observed.

"I do," he agreed, his eyes not leaving hers.

She exhaled loudly and looked away, not ready to have that conversation right now.

"I still don't think…"

He held up a hand to cut her off.

"It's not for everyone. It might not be for you. God knows, with your mother…"

"Hey!" Heidi protested. "Just because she believes strongly in women's rights…"

"True or false? She commonly refers to straight white men as 'our oppressors'?"

Heidi winced and blew out a breath. "True," she admitted.

"True or false? She considers labeling restrooms as 'Women's and Men's' a form of 'gender apartheid'."

Heidi sighed. "Also true. You know it is."

"Mmmhmm. And she has a right to her opinions, but just consider how they might influence your perception of your hot, intriguing, *protective* neighbor," he said, a teasing glint in his eye. "Speaking of whom, do you think you'll see him again?"

"Probably tonight," Heidi mumbled. "I took the train in today, and I think he's taking me to get my car when I get home."

Paul focused on this.

"So maybe you could suggest doing something this weekend, to thank him!"

"Can't. No, really," she insisted, when Paul looked at her skeptically. "Not only do I have a ton of work to do, *legitimately*, but I actually, um… promised my mom I'd visit." She shrugged sheepishly.

Paul sighed.

"Well, if it's meant to be, an opportunity will present itself. Just… keep an open mind," he advised as he stood up and stretched.

Heidi figured that wouldn't be a problem. Right now her mind was flooded with all the things Paul had told her, and all the things she still wanted to know.

"We have got to get some decent furniture in here," Paul complained, and Heidi's attention snapped back to the present.

"If only I had an executive assistant I could delegate a task like that to…" she mused.

Paul grinned and handed her the FedEx envelope with a mock salute.

"I'm on it, boss."

Chapter 6

*D*addy's little sex kitten.

Dom groaned out loud, scrolling through the profile pics on *Fetforyou*.

The blonde looked like she was barely out of college, wearing a hot pink tank that rose several inches above her navel, skin-tight leggings, and dangling a pacifier from her index finger while giving the camera a raucous wink.

Shit.

Surely the owners of the site planted actresses or models to lure in the singles.

One could hope.

He'd always been lucky. Brother to Boston's most eligible dominant, he'd ridden Matteo's coattails and always managed to find someone in the scene pretty easily. He would walk into pretty much any club, and could be guaranteed to walk out with a girl on his arm. So he shouldn't have been surprised that when he got into the scene in Boston—some underground, more exclusive, and hidden, but some rather overt and open—there were single women at the ready. There had been a boom in interest ever since the romance industry found the sweet spot in the whole Dom/sub sub-genre, and to Dom's relief, many were just curious, or looking to test things out.

He raised an eyebrow at the next profile pic. Were those tattooed eyebrows? He frowned. He was all for 'live and let live', but the whole black ensemble and full-body piercing wasn't his kink.

Turning his head to the side, he tried to figure out the next picture. Was that a man, or a woman? Yikes.

There were many submissives in the local area. But none were what he was looking for.

What *was* he looking for?

It wasn't until he discarded the profile of a perfectly attractive, professional-looking woman with short, curly hair, that it dawned on him.

Full, thick, long hair the color of melted chocolate. Piercing blue eyes that changed like the crashing waves of the ocean, eyes that could be calm and welcoming, or stormy and foreboding. Fetching freckles across the nose, a pouty mouth, a full figure that beckoned to be touched…

She was on his mind because he was still awaiting her text.

Period.

His phone buzzed, and he glanced quickly. How late did that girl work, anyway? When the hell was she going to text him? Did she think he sat around day waiting for her text?

Tony calling.

He picked up the phone on the second ring, though he well knew a phone call from his youngest brother most certainly meant he was looking for something.

"Yeah," Dom said, not wasting time or breath on pleasantries.

"'Sup, man," Tony said on the other line. "What are you up to?"

"Oh, just scrolling through the sordid, somewhat terrifying profile pics on *Fetforyou*," Dom said. "You?"

"For real?"

Dom sighed. "For real."

"What happened to that chick you were taking home?"

"Didn't work out," Dom said shortly. Tony, though well informed of the scene that both Matteo and Dom lived, wasn't into the scene himself. No need to give him the gory details.

"Sorry."

Dom snorted, as he remembered the scathing texts Tammy had sent him.

You call yourself a dom? I've gotten better spankings from my sorority sisters.

Hell hath no fury like a submissive scorned.

"Don't be," he said.

"Dom, seriously, man, why not try out vanilla again? Maybe pick up a girl at a bar, like normal guys do? This is the Hub, you know? Gorgeous girls everywhere you go."

"Yeah," Dom said with a sigh. "Not sure I can do vanilla."

He *liked* being in control. He liked the sense of power and the eroticism of it all. He didn't do flowers and hearts and *romance*.

"Sounds like you're not doing much of anything," Tony countered.

Dom growled. "So you called just to give me shit about my love life?"

"Uh, no," Tony said. Figured. "We, uh, have kind of an issue here." He spoke quickly, getting it all out in once sentence. "Val maxed out the damn credit card at the shoe convention at Copley, and now I'm coming up short, and electricity rates are up here, and—"

"Why do you allow her to do that?" Dom interrupted, his anger rising. Tony's girlfriend, Valerie, was a spender, and Tony had spoiled the girl by getting her anything she wanted. She was always dressed to the nines, with perfectly manicured nails and the latest bags and shoes. Valerie was a sweet girl, but really needed to stop spending all of Tony's money, and it pissed both Dom and Matteo off that Tony wouldn't man up and stop her.

"Dom, this is the modern era. I don't *allow* or *forbid* anything, despite what archaic ideas you and Matteo have about shit."

"Archaic my ass," Dom growled, not sure what he wanted to do more; shake some sense into the girl spending his brother's hard-earned money like water, or shake his brother, who allowed the stupidity. "You don't have to be a cave man to protect what's yours."

He meant to refer to Tony's money. Tony owned an Italian restaurant in town, *Cara*, in the North End, and did well for himself. Still, the restaurant business was fickle, with serious competition downtown, and income wasn't always steady. He had large bills to pay, and his spendy girlfriend didn't help. But as Dom spoke, his own words conjured up an image of Heidi, leaning on his arm, a look of pain on her face as he instinctively laced a hand around her waist.

You don't have to be a cave man to protect what's yours.

"I don't want to get into it, Dom," Tony muttered. "I'll talk to Val. Promise. And it's not all her fault, either. Sales are down this month, and I wasn't planning on having to replace the stove so soon." Tony had inherited a fully functional kitchen when he'd purchased the restaurant, and to his surprise, the stove on his industrial oven had to be replaced much sooner than he'd anticipated.

"This will be the last time," Tony promised.

"What do you need?"

As Dom and Tony discussed details—and Tony's request ended up being much less than Dom had anticipated—Dom glanced out the window. He almost dropped the phone.

Was that Heidi? With that little mutt of hers on a leash? He flicked the shade and noticed her stop at her car, open the driver's side door and retrieve something, then shut the door and turn, walking toward his apartment.

What the hell?

Her *car?*

"Is that all right?" Tony said on the other line. Dom had vaguely been aware of a mention of Tony stopping by the next day.

"Yeah, fine," he said. "I'll talk to you in the morning. I gotta go."

"Thanks, man," Tony said, and a click indicated he'd hung up. Dom all but flung his cell on his couch as he stalked to his door.

What was she doing walking her dog? And how did she get her car back? For the love of…

He opened the door before she even rang the bell.

Her wide blue eyes looked startled as he yanked the door open, her finger still poised over the bell. Her lips formed a perfect little 'O' and he almost forgot he was pissed. Almost.

"Is that your car over there?" he asked evenly, crossing his arms over his chest and frowning at her.

A flush crept over her cheeks and her eyes flashed.

"It is."

"We had a plan," he bit out. "I've been waiting for your text for the past—" did he really want to admit he'd been waiting all day?—"hour. And now I look out my window and see your car!" He threw up his hands in exasperation. "I told you to call me!"

Her little dog pulled on the leash, and when he did, Heidi winced. Dom felt a pang of guilt.

"I *tried* to," she said as she yanked back on the leash. "I messaged you two times and for some odd reason, the message wouldn't go through." She reached into her pocket for her phone, and another spasm of pain crossed her face. Dom felt like an ass. Was he supposed to invite her in? Would she think that creepy? Send her home so she could rest? But before he could decide what to do next, her dog pulled again on the leash and flew past him, between his legs, and into his apartment.

"Princess!" Heidi hissed.

"I'll get her," Dom said, not caring about the little dog so much as the fact that Heidi looked like she was going to pass out right there on his step. "Come here," he ordered, reaching out to take her arm firmly, placing another hand on her waist and practically lifting her over his stoop. He half-carried, half-led her to the brown leather couch in his living room.

He realized with a quick beat of his heart that his laptop was still open.

Shit. Had she seen what was on the screen? But no, she couldn't; the screen saver was on now, and her eyes were trained to the entryway to the kitchen, where her little dog was rummaging around. He nestled her on the sofa, took two large strides over to his desk, and slammed the lid on his laptop closed before heading toward the kitchen.

The dog was in his recycling. He barely stifled a growl. Between irritation that Heidi got her car and didn't ask him, and annoyance that the stupid dog was in his recycling, he wasn't feeling like the most hospitable neighbor.

"Stop!" The dog dropped the empty egg carton she was wrestling and looked up, blinking at him.

Good to know at least one member of the female population did what she was told.

And he would've had the whole situation in control—just as he liked it—if Heidi hadn't piped up from the other room.

"Princess! Get in here, you little—" Princess broke eye contact with Dom, snatched something shiny and much too large for her tiny mouth, and bolted past Dom toward Heidi. Dom grunted, gathering up the papers and empty cans scattered across his kitchen floor.

"Oh gosh, Dom, I'm so sorry," Heidi said, sounding flustered from the other room. "She's such a little stinker. Doesn't do a thing I tell her. She was spoiled rotten before I got her, and now she—*Princess, give me that*—thinks she can do whatever she—oh!" She paused. "Oh, my," she murmured to herself. Dom turned, knee deep in recycling, and turned to see why Heidi had paused mid-sentence.

Holy shit.

Princess had snatched the *Flog-her.com* catalog from the recycling.

Why did they even *send* that incriminating shit?

He was done being taken off guard. Done not having a handle on the situation. Done feeling out of control. This wasn't who he was. This wasn't how he did things. He was a fucking dominant, and doms took control of the situation.

Turning back to the recycling as if he hadn't seen her look through the catalog, he made sure everything was perfectly fine, then walked nonchalantly back into the living room. Heidi had dropped the catalog, a decided flush creeping along her neck and cheeks, and she was blinking rapidly.

He was going to get control back. *Now.*

The catalog would stay exactly where it was.

"Can I get you a drink?" he asked, as if the catalog on her lap wasn't filled with pictures of paddles, floggers, and canes, the cover girl bent enticingly over a large desk remarkably like the one right behind Heidi. He acted as if she held a men's clothing catalog, or perhaps a little advertisement from the British Tea Company.

She blinked and swallowed.

"Water?" she croaked.

Princess moved, causing Heidi to shift and wince. He turned a stern eye to the dog and pointed his index finger.

"Stay!" he ordered. Princess dropped her head to her paws and sighed.

He leaned against arm of the couch and folded his arms across his chest.

"We have some things to discuss," he stated, fully in control of the situation. Heidi's eyes flicked back down to the catalog in her lap. "But first, I asked if you need something to drink. Something stronger than water?"

"Water would be good," she murmured. "Thank you."

He gave a curt nod, and walked to the kitchen. He would take his time, as he was curious what she'd do with the catalog. Tapping the ice tray on the counter, he glanced out of the corner of his eye to see what she was doing. He barely stifled a chuckle. She was fully immersed in the catalog.

Could be nothing but morbid curiosity, but his hunch said otherwise.

He poured a glass of water, turned, and stalked back to the living room. As he anticipated, when he entered the living room, her eyes flew back up, pretending she hadn't been perusing the spanking implements in the catalog in her lap.

"Oh, hey, I'll take that," he said nonchalantly, reaching his hand out. She flushed again. Damn, she looked hot when she flushed. Her eyes grew brighter, her cheeks more pronounced, even her chest was heaving. As she reached her hand out, he wondered exactly why she blushed. Was it understandable embarrassment? Or something more? It appeared some probing was in order.

He really had to do something about the stupid catalog that came in the mail. Should've tossed it in the garbage instead of the recycling. Dom knew what he liked and had a ready supply of tools he ordered from a private contractor online. The catalog had been a gag gift for Christmas from Matteo.

Dom took a long, deliberate look at the cover, as if he were just now realizing what it was. He barely tempered a grin, looking at the Fabio-like dominant with a stern look on his face, wide paddle in hand, repentant striped bottom looming beneath him. It was so over-the-top it was comical. "Oh, this stupid thing," he said, as he pushed himself to his feet and walked toward the recycling. He snorted. "My brother thought it would be funny to send me this for Christmas." He tossed it into the bin. "I don't have any use for that shit," he tossed over his shoulder.

It was the God's honest truth. He much preferred the custom-made tools he ordered over the factory-made crap. Still, he wanted to keep her wondering.

"Oh," she said. He turned back to her, and smiled.

She smiled back. Shit, she was beautiful. But he had a matter to tend to.

Heidi was not his submissive. He was not her dominant. However, he'd given her a specific instruction, and it wasn't something he could ignore, no matter what their relationship. If she were his, he'd punish her for it. She wasn't. And he wouldn't. But he'd make damn sure she knew he wasn't happy with the fact she'd not done what she was told.

Why did girls *do* that?

She could've gotten herself into an accident, or hurt herself worse. All she had to do was message him. He'd been right there, waiting the whole time. He felt himself growing stern.

"Now tell me why you got your car after I told you to message me so I could help you get it."

Her eyes widened and she swallowed. Good. He wanted her to feel his displeasure. He wanted her to know he disliked being disobeyed.

She thrust her pretty chin in the air, as if she'd just gotten braver.

"I wanted to," she said stubbornly. He felt his eyes narrow but she went on. "I appreciate all your help, Dom," she said, "I really, really do."

Princess raised her head. Dom gave her a stern look and pointed back to Heidi's lap. The dog obediently put her head back down. Heidi swallowed, but met Dom's eyes. "But I..." Her voice lowered as she spoke. "I got a taxi and had them bring me to the gym. I-I..." she stammered again and it pleased him to know his sternness flustered her. He kept his gaze fixed on her. "I didn't want to bother you any more."

He frowned. "I asked you to text me," he said. "Why didn't you at least text me?"

"As I said," she continued, with measured words, "I *tried* to. But the messages came back."

Frowning at her phone, he beckoned silently for her to hand it to him. Her eyes narrowed, but she obeyed.

He glanced at the message she supposedly tried to send him. *Message undelivered.*

"You sent it to the wrong number."

"Maybe you *gave* me the wrong number," she retorted.

He felt his anger rising. This girl!

With a growl, he entered his number in her phone and in the 'text' portion, wrote 'DOM'. He hit send, for once in his life thankful his mother had given him the name she did, grateful the message on Heidi's phone would be clear as hell.

"There. Now you have my number. And I wouldn't have made the offer if it inconvenienced me."

"But you've done enough," she argued. He felt his hackles go up. He was not in the mood to argue. Her eyes grew heated, and he wasn't sure why, but she pushed on. "And although I appreciate your help, I'm fully capable of taking care of myself."

"I never said you weren't."

Her eyes flashed. "I hardly know you!" she protested.

"Easily remedied," he countered, allowing his eyes to travel to her sitting propped up on his couch. He paused, making sure she felt the full weight of his words. "But there's something you need to know, Heidi." He paused to make sure he had her attention as he leaned forward.

"I always mean what I say."

She swallowed, and the fight went out of her. "Well, yeah," she whispered. "Sorry."

He gave a curt nod. Forgiven. If she were his, it would be a different story.

"You feeling better?" he asked.

"Better than I did this morning."

"You need to avoid the gym for a few days. And can you take work off?"

She shook her head. "Not really, but I should be able to work from home a day or two. I don't have a meeting with a client until the end of the week."

He nodded approvingly. "Good," he said, barely restraining himself from attaching *girl* to the end. *Good girl*, his mind said.

She looked so tired. The day's events had likely drained her, and she needed some rest.

"You need some sleep," he murmured. Her eyes flicked to his couch and the blanket slung casually over the armrest.

Not yet, honey.

"I'll help you back," he said.

"All right," she said, and her shoulders drooped. Poor girl. He wanted to lay her down on the couch and tuck that blanket around her. Watch her while she slept. Make sure she didn't hurt herself when she went to shower, or get herself something to eat.

He stood in front of her. She placed her glass on the small end table next to the couch, and she reach for his proffered hand. When she did, he felt it again, her small, fragile hand in his large one. It was a feeling he could get used to, the most chaste but welcome touch. She stood with difficulty, and he put his arm around her waist. She felt so soft and feminine, and being in such close proximity, he could smell the faint, intoxicating scent of her, something citrusy and vibrant, spicy, and altogether enchanting.

With Princess under one arm, and Heidi all but under the other, he walked her carefully to her apartment.

"Hand me your keys," he ordered outside her door, and she complied. He pushed the door open, went to flick the entryway light, and noticed it didn't light up.

"It's broken," she explained. "I called the building manager last week, but—"

"I'll take care of it in the morning," he said, as he pushed the door open and led her over the stoop. Damn the lazy-ass building manager.

She sighed. "You don't have to—"

Why did she have to argue over everything?

"Heidi," he warned, all patience now gone.

She didn't respond.

He deposited Princess in the living room and pointed to her dog bed in the hallway. "Go," he ordered. Princess trotted off.

He stood and shifted his arm around Heidi again, helping her onto her couch.

"You get some rest," he said, feeling the desire rise again to take care of her, tuck her in, help her into her nightclothes and soothe her to sleep. "And tomorrow morning, I'll check in on you. You've got my number now," he said. "You need anything, you text me. Got it?"

She lifted smiling blue eyes to him. God, those eyes.

"I will," she said. "And Dom, thank you."

"No problem," he said, turning to let himself out, barely tempering his instinctive desire to protect her. "You be a good girl and get some rest now."

As he opened the door, he could almost see it, Heidi, kneeling before him, her little hands placed trustingly in his lap, looking up at him with those wide blue eyes, eager to please, his to command. He could almost hear her, the purr-like compliance of her voice whispering *Yes, sir,* to an instruction he'd given her.

But that was the stuff of fantasies. For all he knew, she'd

revolt at the mere thought of submitting to him, and any interest he'd taken as a green light was nothing more than curiosity, or even revulsion.

Why don't you go back to vanilla for a while?

He had to be real. Had to get himself out of fantasy and back to reality.

Enough with this shit.

Chapter 7

The drumming was invading her brain. *Boom boom ba dum, boom boom ba dum…*

Heidi had always figured that her ability to focus on a task despite all distractions was kind of her superpower. Yeah, it wasn't as useful as mind reading, or as sexy as, say, having super-bendy legs, but, it had gotten her through high school and the drama of her parents' not-at-all-amicable breakup without losing her valedictorian status. It had helped her earn a BS with high honors in just three years, despite her roommate's nocturnal schedule and love of parties. It had always been a solid, dependable sort of superpower, the kind she could use for good and not for evil.

Until today. She'd finally met her nemesis, and its name was meditation drumming.

"It's *so perfect* for improving your concentration and helping you really channel your creativity," her mother had enthused as she'd turned up the stereo, looking entirely too bright-eyed for a woman who had sworn off coffee a decade ago. "You remember Peggy, that friend of mine from North Adams who makes the wool art? She swears by it."

And then her mother had turned and disappeared into the garage-turned-workshop, her long brown braid flying out behind her, leaving Heidi to endure the auditory assault alone.

After what felt like hours, Heidi could confirm that her creativity had definitely been channeled. She'd already contemplated several methods of destroying her mother's ancient sound system.

"Mom, can you turn that down?" she finally called towards the door to the garage.

No answer. *Typical*. Her mother probably couldn't even hear the music from out there.

Suppressing a groan, Heidi dropped the sheaf of financial records she'd been attempting to review back on the tabletop and massaged her aching head. If the music didn't drive her batty, dealing with this client was going to.

Fifty-seven thousand dollars a year, Heidi thought, shaking her head. That was the going rate for tuition at the prestigious Easterbrook Academy. Considering their unbelievable test scores and the fact that only a handful of their 104 graduates last year *didn't* make it into an Ivy League school, she figured they could get away with charging that much. But only if the scandal involving the departure of two formerly well respected board members stayed hushed up.

Easterbrook prided itself on being a school that accepted the best and brightest—only the most ambitious and academically gifted applicants were selected, which was why an Easterbrook diploma was worth the price of several mid-sized SUVs. And, proud alumni could be counted on to provide annual donations that ensured even those applicants whose parents couldn't afford the staggering tuition were able to attend. At least, that's how it was supposed to work... until a pair of board members had been caught accepting bribes disguised as alumni support—'gifts' from affluent alumni to guarantee their children admission, regardless of academic proficiency.

To the credit of the remaining board members, once the problem had been discovered, they'd made sure the bribe money had quickly been returned, and the two guilty members had been quickly voted out. But that hadn't solved the problem. Easterbrook was left with an enormous deficit in their alumni grant budget, several deserving students without funds to pay their tuition for the coming year, and no way to make up the shortfall without going public and damaging the school's reputation. After months of bickering, the board had been unable to solve the problem, and decided they needed an impartial consultant. Now it was up to Heidi and Paul to bridge the gap or cut the budget.

It would be a hell of a lot easier if the inefficient, downright unhelpful *administrators* of Easterbrook would realize that they were all on the same team!

Heidi sighed and stood up, stretching her still-aching back. She walked over to turn the stereo off before turning to look around the cluttered kitchen. The table, with its pattern of blue and white Mexican tiles, was familiar. She'd sat in that very chair a dozen years ago while her Dad reviewed her math homework and her mother cooked dinner... back then, it would've been something *normal*, with meat and gluten.

The rest of the kitchen was absolutely nothing like the home she remembered. Gone were the empty counters and organized cabinets her mother had once prized. Now, every surface was covered with an ever-changing jumble of ingredients for her mother's candle- and soap-making business: half-filled mason jars and scraps of fabric, apothecary jars of dried herbs and flowers, vials of essential oils and extracts. The table now sat perpendicular to the back door, to allow for better energy flow, and tacked to practically every square inch of the sunny yellow walls were calls to 'Say No to GMO!' 'Feed the Poor, Don't Fund the War!' and 'Reject Gender Discrimination!'

Heidi recalled this last poster well. Her mother had carried it while protesting, topless, outside a local college football stadium that didn't provide adequate facilities for women, and she'd brought her (fully-clothed) teen-aged daughters along to witness grassroots activism firsthand. Heidi didn't remember very much about the actual protest... but, she could recount word-for-word the epic showdown between her parents afterward.

"You show your tits to whomever you like, Frances, I can't stop you. But no daughter of mine is going to hang around with a bunch of half-naked stoners who are just begging to be arrested on public indecency charges!" Her mild-mannered, indifferent father had been apoplectic for once.

"You don't *own* me, Charles! You don't *own* these girls! You don't own our *breasts* or control our *sexuality*! You should be outraged at the rampant gender inequality your daughters have to face!"

Heidi shook her head at the memory. *Happy times.*

From beneath the pile of papers, her phone dinged with a new text message, and just like that, the sour reminder of her parents' imploding marriage evaporated and her stomach flipped in anticipation.

How quickly I've been conditioned, she thought wryly as she dug out the phone and sat down, pushing all of her paperwork aside. She smiled when she saw the incoming message from Dom.

Morning, sunshine.

She quickly typed, *Good morning!*

Staying out of trouble?

Though she hadn't seen Dom for three and a half days, *not that she was counting*, she'd become accustomed to his frequent 'check-in' texts. She'd almost convinced herself that it was nothing more than a neighborly gesture, making sure that her back was healthy after that stupid incident at the gym. But then... her back had gotten better, and the texts had continued. What did *that* mean? Were they... friends?

'How are you feeling?' and 'Let me know if you need anything' had somehow become 'Text me when you get to your mother's house' and 'Tell me you weren't speeding, Heidi'. It was ridiculous, of course—a grown woman driving familiar roads in broad daylight shouldn't have to check in with anyone. Her mother would say his demands were borderline-stalker.

Heidi could only think that they felt... nice.

It was *nice* to know someone was concerned that she arrived at her destination and that she had gotten herself there safely. It was *nice* that someone had noticed her broken light and had coerced the building manager into fixing it the very next day. It was *nice* to know that someone was waiting for her to come back. It was *nice* that...

Heidi? Everything okay?

It was nice that someone cared.

Yeah, hi! I'm still here!

Good. How's everything going?

Heidi bit her lip for a moment, contemplating her answer. Things were going... the way they usually went with her mother.

When Heidi had arrived yesterday morning, her mother had been delighted to see her and had plied her with questions about her new apartment and business. She'd been genuinely thrilled to hear how successful Heidi's business was becoming... though she couldn't pretend to summon any real enthusiasm for the actual work Heidi did, since the concept of financial auditing held the taint of 'Big Corporate', which her mother was *firmly* against. She'd made Heidi tea and enlisted her support with wrapping candles for display at the Down East Flea Market yesterday afternoon.

And then just a few hours after Heidi's arrival, someone named Molly had called about a rally against refugees... or was it *for* refugees? Whichever. In any case, it was a *crisis*, Molly said, and did Frances have time to lend a hand? Which was a silly question, because, *of course*, Frances had time to save the world one refugee at a time, and she'd gone off to do just that, leaving

Heidi with a rapidly brewing headache and a bunch of pungently scented candles to wrap.

But that wasn't the sort of thing you shared with a casual friend in a text. Or at all.

Fine!

Just… fine?

Wrapped some candles, reviewed some paperwork for a client, endured an hour of aboriginal drumming… The usual family stuff.

That's the usual family stuff, huh?

Heidi grinned.

Yup. Isn't that what you do with your family?

This may shock you, but my brothers don't appreciate the art of candle wrapping.

Heidi tucked her tongue into her cheek.

That's so sad! You're really missing out.

Yet somehow we get by.

She could almost hear his dry, mocking tone.

So, what do you do instead?

One of my brothers always has some DIY project going on, so we generally load up on power tools and take care of business.

Wow. That sounds… manly.

We're men, so… yeah.

Hmmm… Do you get all sweaty doing that kind of thing?

Sure, sometimes.

So… you all probably have to take your shirts off?

There was a pause, which turned Heidi's smile into a full grin.

Sometimes.

Your brother? He's the guy from the gym, right?

A longer pause this time, which made Heidi smile even wider.

Yeah. That's one of them.

And… does your other brother look like you two?

This pause lasted a full half-minute, by which time Heidi was giggling.

Tony? More or less. Why?

I'm just trying to get a visual of you three… with power tools.

You know what? I'd rather you didn't imagine my brothers half naked.

Heidi bit her lip and stared at her phone. Did that mean he wouldn't mind her visualizing *him* half-naked?

And then suddenly she *was* visualizing him half-naked and *ohmygod* was it warm in here? She remembered his brother had those tattoos all over his arms, and wondered whether Dom had any ink, maybe hiding underneath his…

A hand waving in front of her face made her jump, and her phone flew out of her hand, clattering onto the tabletop.

"Yeesh, Heidi! Where did your mind wander off to?" Her sister Hillary shook her head in amusement, sending her short auburn hair sliding around her face.

Heidi pressed a hand to her chest as her heart resumed beating, and fixed her sister with a narrow-eyed glare.

"God, Hillie! Have nearly four years of college made you completely forget your manners? It's customary to say 'hello' rather than sneaking up on a person and scaring years off her life."

Hillary laughed and set a Starbucks coffee cup down on the table.

"I already said hi and told you I'd come home to do laundry! I've been talking to you for two full minutes and I only *just* realized that you haven't been paying attention! You've been too busy giggling and talking to…"

Hillary grabbed for the phone before Heidi could reach for it.

"Ahhh… to *Dom*… who apparently doesn't like you imagining his brothers half-naked?" Hillary asked, waggling her eyebrows suggestively. "Are they hot?"

Heidi felt herself flush and held out her hand imperiously.

"Give me back my phone, demon spawn! And don't make this out to be something it's not. It's… he's just a friend."

"Hmmm…" Hillary said, turning away from Heidi's outstretched hand and quickly scrolling up the page to read the previous messages. "Sounds like a very *concerned* friend! 'Don't forget to call me when you get there'."

She turned back to fix Heidi with a speculative look.

"Who *is* this guy, Heidi?"

"Are you seriously reading my private messages?" Heidi said, standing up from the table in outrage. "Don't be obnoxious! And I told you—"

Hillary waved airily.

"Yes, yes, you told me," Hillary said with a gloating smile and a glint in her light blue eyes. She pushed Heidi gently back into her chair and pulled out a chair for herself. "Now, tell me *more.*"

Heidi counted to ten and prayed for patience. Hillary was, by far, the best gift her parents had ever given her. Thoughtful, tenderhearted, fun. But seemingly from the cradle, Hillie had had this compulsive need to believe in *love*—the Disney, hearts-and-flowers, someday-my-prince-will-come, and-they-lived-happily-ever-after kind of love. The fairy tale. That she had weathered their parents' divorce with that belief still so firmly intact was absurd… and wonderful.

With a resigned sigh, Heidi asked, "What do you want to know?"

"Well, first things first. Drink your coffee," Hillary commanded, tucking a strand of hair behind her ear and nudging the coffee cup closer to Heidi. "I figured mom would have you drinking that crappy green tea."

The coffee was barely warm, but it was *not* crappy green tea. Heidi took a grateful sip, feeling her taste buds explode from the combination of vanilla flavoring and sugar. Her mother's insistence on eating vegan, sustainable foods free of sugar and preservatives at least had the side benefit of ensuring that Heidi wasn't tempted to overindulge during her visits. Sticking to a 1200-calorie-a-day diet was positively easy when she spent time at her mother's house.

"Okay, now..." Hillary continued, with an expression on her face that said Christmas had come early, as far as she was concerned. "What does this mystery man *look* like?"

"Well..." Heidi lifted the coffee cup to hide the smile that instinctively sprang to her lips. It was important that Hillary not get the wrong idea. "He's medium height... ah... medium build... um... he shaves his head..." She trailed off and shrugged, as though she hadn't cataloged every one of Dom's features and replayed them all in her head, over and over, from his electric green eyes, to his lean, muscular arms, and even the way his bare feet had looked when he'd bent down to pet Princess...

God, she had it bad.

Hillary looked disappointed at Heidi's casual assessment, but she rallied.

"Okay, so... how did you meet?"

"He lives next door," Heidi answered innocently. "I pulled my back at the gym and he helped me home, and we exchanged numbers, just in case I needed anything." Heidi indicated the cell phone Hillary still clutched.

"He's just... a nice guy!" Heidi finished, trying not to laugh at Hillary's pout.

"Who's a nice guy?" Frances asked, as she walked into the kitchen with an enormous cardboard box and set it on the counter with a rattle.

Heidi sighed. *Perfect.*

"My next door neighbor," Heidi said quickly, figuring that the fewer details she gave her mother, the less ammunition she'd have.

Hillary, the traitor, clearly did not agree.

"She's been texting him," Hillary confided. "Flirty texts."

Heidi shot Hillary a look of disbelief.

"They're *not* flirty. I hurt my back the other day and he just texted to ask how I was feeling," Heidi lied, shooting her sister a warning glare, daring her to reveal more.

Hillary pressed her lips together and said nothing.

"Hmmm…" their mother said, glancing warily from Heidi to Hillary. "Be careful, sweetie. You know how men try to take advantage when they think a girl is weak. Give them an inch—a *millimeter*—and they'll try to control your every move."

"I know, Mom," Heidi said wearily.

"There was a time," their mother continued, resting her hands atop the box and staring blankly out the window, "when I thought your father was just a nice guy. Once he got me where he wanted me, he forgot that I existed, as long as I cleaned his house and cooked his dinner. Like I wasn't a human being! Like I didn't have my own dreams and plans…"

Heidi narrowed her eyes at Hillary in a silent message. *Thanks a bunch. Now you've got her started.*

Hillary's mouth twisted in a silent reply. *Shit. Sorry.*

"And just look how *that* ended," Frances continued. "The minute I tried to have a life outside of *his* home, *his* hobbies, *his* career, he showed his true colors!"

"Mom, I was just teasing Heidi," Hillary interrupted, standing up from the table and going to put her arm around their mother's shoulders. "Don't get all worked up. "

And then, before their mother could protest, Hillary steered her toward the garage. "Why don't you show me those new candles you're working on for the summer?" she said with credible enthusiasm.

When their mother had stepped into the garage, Hillary ducked back and slid something onto the table in front of Heidi. Her phone! She'd almost forgotten!

"I flipped it to silent," Hillary said quickly, glancing towards the garage. "But it's been vibrating in my hand for the past five

minutes. Your *friend* must be dying to know about your back...
Babe."

"Hillie?" their mother called.

"Coming, Mom!"

And with a wink and a smile that was just a little *too* knowing,
Hillary jogged back to the garage, leaving Heidi with the
phone... and a knot in her stomach that wasn't from anticipation. She glanced at the screen and saw that she'd missed three
messages.

Heidi?

Babe, you'd better not be thinking about my brothers.

Hello?

What the heck was she doing here? She had friends... and
none of them texted randomly to check on her the way Dom
did. God, *Paul* hadn't texted her *once* this weekend, and *he* was
dog-sitting Princess! None of her other friends called her 'Babe'.
And for sure, none of them cared if she ogled their brothers.
Hillary was right about one thing... It *was* flirty. And it seemed to
be mutual.

Heidi tapped her fingernail on the tabletop and stared hard
at the phone.

So... what was she hoping would happen? She wasn't naive
enough to think that she could have a relationship with Dom that
didn't include... kinky aspects. That part was actually kind of...
well, *very* intriguing. Her mind helpfully replayed the sound of
Tammy's cry of pleasure, and she felt an answering pulse low in
her belly. *Yes.* Yes, she definitely wanted that.

But, Dom... being in control was a requirement for him. And
she had a feeling that control wouldn't just be about where she
could put her hands or when she was allowed to speak in bed.
How much control would he expect? How much was she willing
—or able—to give? And, most importantly, would it even be
worth the risk? As she worried this over, the phone vibrated in
her hands.

Okay, I'm guessing the candle wrapping or the drumming have got your attention. If you need me, let me know. I'll be here.

He'd be there if she needed him.

Such a small thing, almost a throwaway comment, but even though she'd only really known him for three and a half days... she believed that he meant it.

And just like that, she knew. With a shuddering breath, she typed.

Dom... I really like you.

She followed that with another text.

Just wanted you to know that.

There was no response. One minute passed, then two, and her confidence eroded like sand in the tide.

Shit. What a stupid, stupid thing to do. I sound like a lovesick middle-schooler. He was her neighbor. He had a cavalcade of gorgeous, svelte, busty women parading through his front door every single day... she was *not* his type. What must he think of her for... Her phone vibrated.

When are you coming back?

God. What did *that* mean? He knew that she was planning to go back tomorrow morning, right before work. He'd asked her that before. Did he want her to come back early? Suddenly she needed to *know*, for once and for all.

Tonight. I decided I'm coming back tonight.

Good. Come to me as soon as you get home.

A fiery coil that was half excitement and half fear shivered up her spine and spread warmth through her stomach, even as the phone vibrated once more.

And, Heidi... drive safely.

Boom boom ba dum, Boom boom ba dum... Not freakin' meditation drumming this time, but the crazy, excited pounding of Heidi's own heart.

Chapter 8

She was on her way home.

He'd lost all sense of propriety and fucking *ordered* her to come to him.

Dom was vaguely aware of a sense of foreboding, something in him that said *turn back now, before it's too late,* but he ignored it. He didn't cave to fear, and what fun was a relationship that was safe and predictable?

He shouldn't be so happy to have her come home, when he'd only known her for three days.

Should he?

She'd messaged that she liked him, making him feel like a teen again.

She likes me!

He'd grinned at the message when it came in.

It had been so long since he'd shown interest in a girl other than someone at The Club. Though the girls from The Club wanted stern and bossy, most would assume it was an act of sorts. But with Heidi, he'd been himself. He'd even let his guard down. And she hadn't sent him scathing messages telling him to mind his own damn business. No, she'd done the opposite. She told him she liked him.

As he was.

She wasn't a pushover, either—she did like to hold her ground, and he found he liked that about her.

Where was the challenge, if she was putty in his hands?

Then what was it that tugged on his conscience? He shook his head as he unloaded his dishwasher, and began putting things away. And as he slid the heavy glasses to the back of the cabinet, he probed.

Dom liked to face fear head-on, look it in the eye, and defeat it. He did not bury fear. He wasn't arrogant enough to claim he never *felt* fear. But he would not let it consume him.

So what if this girl appealed to him more than any other girl he'd met in years? So what if her very nearness caused him to grow short of breath, and his pulse pounded when she drew close?

Dom, I really like you.

But he knew she didn't really like him.

She couldn't, because she didn't *know* him. She'd liked what she'd seen so far and yeah, that was cool and hell, he liked her, too. But what would happen when he showed her the real Dom? Would she still *like* him when he laid out his expectation of her obedience? What if she consented? And what if she went running? This wasn't a girl he met at a club or an anonymous chick he met online. This was a girl who lived in the same complex as he did. He'd enjoyed his vacation, despite the looming stress at work he would be returning to shortly, but he would not make a foolish mistake. This wasn't spring break in college.

This was playing with fire.

He could not, *would* not, proceed to do anything without consent. And he wanted her *full* consent, not wide-eyed nodding out of curiosity and attraction to a fantasy belief. He wanted her to know what she was getting into with him.

What *was* she getting into with him?

Just as he finally got to the real source of his fear, his phone buzzed.

He'd asked her to check in with him at every rest stop and tell him where she was.

Five to ten minutes, ETA!

Five minutes? The closest rest stop was an hour away. Where was she messaging from, then? Was she texting while she was driving?

He wasn't sure if the surge of adrenaline he felt was because he suspected she was doing something harebrained and stupid, texting while she drove, or because he only had five minutes to get his shit together before she was home.

He took a deep breath, then exhaled, when a knock came at his door.

Already? Damn.

He shut the dishwasher hard, and went to go open the door, glancing through the glass before he opened it. Mirror-reflection. Matteo.

He yanked the door open.

"Bad timing," Dom grumbled.

Matteo snorted, pushing past Dom to get in, a six-pack in one hand and a brown bag in the other.

"You have a girl in here?" Matteo asked, looking around.

"And if I did?" Dom growled, his eyes zoning in on the bag under Matteo's arm, his stomach growling at the scent.

"I'd push you to try the whole *ménage* thing for once."

Dom glared.

"Dude, chill. I'd leave," Matteo lied. "God, you can be such a tight-ass. So why the bad timing if you don't have a chick?"

"Company coming soon," he said, as his phone buzzed again.

Stuck at construction on Main.

So she *was* texting in the car. They'd talk about that.

Dom held the door open for Matteo and lifted his eyebrows expectantly.

Matteo had the nerve to assume a mock-affronted look. "Moi, Dominic? Your own flesh and blood? Fruit of our parents' loins? We shared the same *womb*. And I can't come and visit? I am deeply offended."

Dom glowered. Matteo grinned.

"Dude, I just stopped by to see if you wanted to catch the game tonight. Picked up something to drink, and some grub. You want me to leave, I'll see myself out," he said, as he moved toward the kitchen. He grabbed a bottle-opener from his key ring and popped the top off a bottle, tossing the top into the trash.

Who got themselves a beer as they were leaving?

Matteo pulled out a chair and straddled it.

Dom narrowed his eyes. "This is leaving?"

"When she comes, I'm outta here," Matteo said, pulling a large takeout tray out of the bag and lifting the lid. "Right now, I'm starving." The aroma of fries and cheeseburgers filled the apartment. Dom's stomach growled. Was that Roadhouse? Shit. He stalked over and grabbed one of the burgers.

"You're evil," he grumbled, the irony of his comment hitting him the minute he took a large bite of the burger. He nearly groaned. Matteo wasn't evil. He was goodness personified. The charbroiled perfection made his mouth water. Matteo well knew Dom's weakness for a Roadhouse burger.

"At your service," Matteo chuckled. The doorbell rang. Matt took several large, crispy fries, and dragged them leisurely through a pile of ketchup on the tray, eyes twinkling, ass staying right where it was, as Dom got to his feet.

He must've been glowering as he yanked the door open, because Heidi's smile froze on her face when she saw him.

"You okay?" she asked, as he gestured her in.

"Yeah," he growled low. "We have company." He led her by

the elbow, which seemed to take her by surprise, as he brought her in and shut the door hard. Matteo's eyes widened when she stepped in, and Dom felt the urge to stand protectively in front of her. Matteo gave a short wave and a friendly grin. She smiled and gave another short wave back.

Dom glared.

She was wearing yoga pants that did wonders for her ass, and a sky blue hoodie that was far too big for her, one side falling off her shoulder. Her hair was pulled back in a cute knobby bun thing, making her look casual, tired, and absolutely gorgeous. God, he was a sucker for the 'girl next door' look.

It was time for his brother to go.

Fortunately, Matteo always inhaled his food and had already eaten most of one of the burgers. Dom picked his burger back up, took a large bite, and glared at Matteo. Matteo dutifully ignored him. It was not lost on Dom that Heidi's eyes were now fixed on the tray of food on the table.

"Hey, you look familiar," Matteo said, as he took another fry, and before Dom could stop him, "You're from The Club, right?"

Dom could've socked him, right then and there, sent him flying on his goddamn ass right across the kitchen.

"Matteo," he growled. Heidi's eyes widened.

"Club?" she blinked. "You guys are in a club?"

To his credit, Matteo immediately realized his error, which worked totally in Dom's favor, because now Matteo was rising to his feet.

"Yeah, um… nah, nothing, just a club Dom and I go to sometimes and I figured maybe that's where I'd seen you," he mumbled. "But I must be wrong." He glanced at the clock on the wall. "Whooee, look at that time!"

"Gym," Heidi said. "You helped me at the gym." Her eyes still wide, she pulled the sweatshirt back up over her shoulder, and as she did, it fell down the other side.

As the realization hit Matteo, he gave Dom an apologetic,

almost childish smile. "Ohhh. Yeah, right. Um, I'll just be going now," he said. Dom's eyes followed him, as Matteo gestured magnanimously. "I'm full now, too," he said. The hell he was. He was a two-double-cheeseburgers-extra-large-fry kinda guy. "Hope you're hungry." She swallowed, eyeing the tray of food. Matteo was already at the door. Dom followed.

"You asshole," Dom hissed. "I haven't had the talk about The Club with her yet."

"I, um, gathered that," Matteo said as his hand hit the door-knob. He turned a shit-eating grin on Dom as the door swung open. "You can kick my ass later. For now, go feed your girl, and if my suspicion is right, which you know it almost always is, you'll thank me later."

Dom responded by shoving his brother out the door and locking it behind him.

He turned to see Heidi staring at him. It looked like she was barely containing her laughter, biting her lip.

He grunted. "Hungry?"

"Starving," she said, looking wistfully at the burgers and fries.

"Help yourself," he said, as he stalked back in the kitchen and pulled a chair out for her. He gestured for her to sit down. She looked down, suddenly bashful.

"Thank you," she murmured.

"Don't thank me," he said, taking another large bite of burger. "Matteo brought the food."

"No, I was thanking you for… never mind," she said. Her eyes watched him chew and swallow. She swallowed again. What the hell?

"Are you gonna eat, or what?" he asked. What was she waiting for?

"Um. Yeah, when I get home," she said. She shook her head. "Sorry. Can't eat this stuff." As he stared at her, she flushed. "Diet," she said in explanation.

He blinked in shock.

"Diet? What the hell are you on a diet for?"

She guffawed. "Um, in case you haven't noticed, Dom, though I do thank you for your ignorance on the matter, I have twenty pounds to lose."

He glared. "The hell you do!"

"I do!" she said, her eyes flashing.

He took a breath. *Here we go again.*

"When's the last time you ate?" he said. And as she paused, he amended. "And I mean *real* food, not whatever hippie shit your mother fed you."

She pursed her lips. "We had... quinoa porridge with flax seeds at nine. And I, um, ate in the car."

"Oh yeah?" he asked, taking another intentionally enormous bite out of his burger. She licked her lips.

He narrowed his eyes. "What'd you eat in the car?"

"A smashed 100-calorie granola bar," she said in a little voice.

He shoved the tray over to her.

"Eat," he ordered, his tone leaving no room for argument. She eyed the food.

"Woman," he warned.

Tentatively, she took a fry and bit into it. Her eyes rolled back and she moaned. Shit. She shouldn't *do* that to him when he was getting stern with her. It affected his concentration.

She took another fry and ate it quickly, then picked up the burger and took a small bite, closing her eyes in utter bliss.

"This is delicious," she moaned. "Ohmigod I'm gonna gain a million pounds but this is gonna be worth it."

"Best burgers in Boston. And don't give me this diet shit," he said. "A burger isn't gonna kill you."

She frowned at him, but he could tell she was oddly pleased.

Club virgin or not, she liked being told what to do. He'd push it a little.

"You're not done until you've eaten at least half that burger," he announced. Her eyes widened. She took another bite.

"Good girl," he said, slowly and deliberately. Her breathing hitched. She swallowed another large bite of burger.

"Oh yeah?" she teased. Her voice had lowered, too, as she leaned forward. "Or what?" she asked innocently.

He gave her the 'behave yourself' look, but she continued to gaze at him speculatively.

"You don't eat your dinner, you won't get the ice cream I have in the freezer."

She gasped. "You'd deny me ice cream as punishment?"

He had a bottle of beer halfway to his lips as her words hung in the air. He grinned around the bottle and took a lazy swig, maintaining eye contact the whole time.

"If you were a naughty girl in need of being punished, then yes," he said evenly. "I would mete out the necessary discipline."

There was no mistaking it now. Her eyes lowered and her breathing was labored. Rubbing her sweaty palms on her yoga pants, she swallowed.

Now was as good a time as any.

He stood, in complete control of the situation. He stacked the trays together. As she stood to help him clean up, he shook his head. "Sit down," he ordered. "I've got this. You must be exhausted after that drive." She frowned.

"I can help," she insisted, reaching for the napkins.

"Ice cream," he growled.

She sat down, a pretty little pout forming on her lips. He barely stifled a chuckle.

"I'm going to finish cleaning up in here. You go get the ice cream, scoop some into a bowl and grab a spoon."

Her eyes widened. "One bowl?" she squeaked.

"One bowl."

"One spoon?" she asked incredulously.

"That's right."

It was all part of his plan.

"Did I not eat enough to earn my dessert?" she asked.

Shit. He'd give her dessert, all right.

He turned and smiled at her. "You did fine, honey," he said. "I'm the one not eating any ice cream."

She frowned. "Why not?"

He shrugged. "I'm on a diet."

She laughed out loud. Her laugh was lovely, unreserved and musical. He grinned at her as she scooped a generous portion of ice cream out. As she put the carton back in the freezer, he picked up the bowl and spoon, took her hand, and led her to the living room.

He loved the feeling of her hand in his.

"Sit down, Heidi," he instructed quietly. She obeyed, tucking her foot under her bottom and leaning back with a sigh of contentment.

"That burger was like eight billion times more satisfying than my mom's sesame tofu stir fry."

"I'd think cardboard sprinkled with salt would be more satisfying than sesame tofu stir fry."

She giggled. "Um, yeah." She reached her hand out for the bowl.

Oh, she was so innocent, it was adorable.

He smiled, but shook his head, as he sat down beside her, taking the bowl in his own hand.

"Do you like games, Heidi?" he asked.

"Um... like strip poker?" she responded. He chuckled.

"Sure, though I don't usually pull that out until at least date three. More like, twenty questions."

She shrugged, eyeing him warily, but the faint flush and deep breathing indicated he'd struck a nerve.

"Let's play a game," he continued. "I ask you a question and if you answer, I'll give you a bite of ice cream."

She bit her lip, smiling. "Okay," she whispered. "May I ask a question before we begin?"

"You may."

"When do I get to ask *my* questions?"

"You get to ask as many questions as you want, any time you want to." And he meant it. He would be honest and forthright, even if it meant she went home tonight and didn't come back. He would tell all, if it killed him.

She nodded, pleased at his response.

"That sounds fair," she whispered.

"You're a good girl," he whispered back. "Question one."

She nodded. His heart began to pound.

"The club Matteo mentioned. Do you have any idea of the kind of club he may be referring to?"

"I think so," she whispered, and squirmed. "Does this have anything to do with the catalog Princess found?"

He nodded. "Very good." He scooped a small bite of ice cream up and fed it to her. She opened her mouth, taking the spoon wholly in, and as he withdrew it, she licked it. His own breath hitched, and he felt himself growing hard. Fucking hell, he loved the control he had over her.

"Have you ever heard of a dominant, Heidi?" he asked, another bite of ice cream held precariously on a spoon in front of her.

She nodded, though her eyes flitted away this time.

"Eyes to me," he ordered.

Her eyes flew back to him. He loved how eager she was to obey.

"Good girl," he crooned. "That earns you two bites."

She clapped her hands like a little girl, licked the spoon again, and it nearly drove him mad.

"Third question. What are your thoughts on the BDSM scene?"

She took a deep breath. "That one deserves an ice cream sundae," she muttered. He chuckled.

"Answer the question, baby," he encouraged. She warmed to

that, her eyes softening, shy even. Maybe a closet baby girl. He would find out, but that was for another day.

"All right. May I ask a question first?"

"Of course."

"Are you a dominant?"

He wasn't expecting her to be so blunt, but he wanted it all out.

"I am."

"Your club is a BDSM club?"

He nodded. "It is."

Her eyes widened and she breathed out. "Whoa."

"Answer the question, Heidi," he chided gently.

"Oh!" she said. "Um. I've read a few books. It sounds—well —" she twisted her hands in her lap. "Really hot," she whispered. "But some sounds *freaky* and I don't think I'm really that kinky and I have never been spanked in my *entire life*. My own parents were all into positive parenting and didn't even do time-outs and definitely not spanking or anything, but I've always kinda wondered… and I. Oh God. Well. You asked," she said, flushing. "I think it sounds hot and scary and exciting," she said all at once.

She was right.

That *did* deserve an ice cream sundae.

"Ice cream," she croaked, reminding him of his end of the bargain as if the ice cream would help her get through the ordeal. He hastened to scoop a bit out and spoon it back into her mouth, and after she swallowed that, he gave her another bite, and another, until the whole damn bowl was empty.

"You didn't eat any," she breathed, licking her lips.

"I can still taste it," he murmured, and before she could catch her breath, he had her in his arms, pulling her onto his lap so that she nestled against one arm, the bowl clattering to the floor forgotten, as he leaned in and took her pouty, adorable, sensual mouth with his own. She tasted so fucking good. He probed, her mouth still cool and creamy from the ice cream, and he heard her moan beneath him as she buckled beneath the heat of his kiss.

"Whoa," she said again, as they pulled away. "Are we still playing?"

He leaned back, as he cradled her against him. "We are," he agreed, still willing to answer any of her questions.

"Do you..." She blushed furiously. "I mean—if your—submissive, they call it?" He nodded, tracing a finger down the length of her shoulder that was once again bared to him. Her breathing grew ragged. "What do you do if your submissive disobeys you?" she said all at once. He chuckled. It was always the first thing a submissive wanted to know.

"Disobedience earns punishment," he explained calmly, aware of the fact that she likely knew this, but hearing him say it was something altogether different... dark, erotic, arousing.

She nodded, eyes wide. "I wish I had more ice cream," she whispered.

He chuckled. "Afraid?"

She nodded.

He held her against his chest, speaking softly into her ear. "Punishment is typically rare," he said. "And everything hinges on your consent."

"So, um... what kind of punishment are we talking about here?" she whispered, as his hand went further down, dipping past her shoulder and to the soft, full, lovely warmth of the skin underneath. The tops of his fingers grazed the top of one soft breast and she gasped, as his thumb moved slowly over her hardened nipple. "Are you... um... talking about no ice cream?" Her voice cracked, and her breath was shallow and labored.

"There are many options a dom has, honey," he said in a low tone. "Personally, I mostly prefer to give a naughty girl a spanking."

She moaned as his thumb circled lazily, her head falling

heavily against his shoulder. "So you," she whispered, her eyes closed now as he continued to tease and caress, "just..." she gulped. "Take them over your lap."

He reached his hand to the other breast, teasing, as he answered slowly. "I've never taken a girl over my lap, no. Spanking over the lap is intimate. I've had them bend over desks, or mostly a bed, sometimes a chair or couch." Her eyes opened, and she nodded.

"What's it like?" she whispered.

"Getting spanked?" He kneaded her breast as she breathed heavily.

"Yes," she whispered.

He shrugged a shoulder. "Spankings hurt, but done right they can also be very, very sexy."

She bit her lip. "Do you use things—like, to—sp-spank with?" she whispered.

He nodded, then paused before he spoke. "I have, but it's not a requirement."

"Thank God," she whispered. He chuckled again.

"Those *things* can make the experience much more erotic," he explained.

"Um, like, what kinds of things? Do you... um, favor?"

He kept eye contact, his hand cupping her breast as he responded. "I tend to favor leather. A strap, or my belt, but I've used many different implements."

Her eyes widened.

"Please stop touching me," she whispered. He immediately withdrew his hand.

She blinked. "I'm sorry. I just... am having a hard time thinking clearly."

He smiled. "Understood. What else do you want to know?"

She bit her lip before speaking. "How does your submissive tell you she's had enough?"

"We have a safeword."

"A safeword?"

He nodded, finally doing what he'd wanted to do so long, running his fingers through her long, soft, gorgeous hair. He sighed. It felt so nice.

"A word we agree on ahead of time, so that if it gets to be too much, you can tell me to stop."

"Okay," she whispered. "So it's all contingent on consent?"

He arranged her on his lap, so she was facing him, his hands on her hips.

"Absolutely," he said with emphasis. "Always." Consent with some of his one-night-stands he'd picked up at The Club had been nebulous. With Heidi, it was imperative.

Her eyes widened. "Always?"

"Always," he promised.

She leaned forward and whispered in his ear.

"Then show me, Dom. Please. I want to know."

He had told the truth when he told her he'd never put a girl over his lap.

Until Heidi, he'd never wanted to.

But when she said, "Show me," he needed to know. What did she want to see?

"Show you what, honey?"

"I want to know what it's like to get spanked," she whispered. And that was all she needed to say. He swung her out, stretching her face down across his thighs as if it were the most natural thing in the world. God, she was gorgeous, and the position, her vulnerability, had him groaning out loud.

"Red, Heidi."

"Red?" she squeaked, her voice lightly muffled. She was squirming as he held her gently in place by applying slight pressure to her lower back.

"That's your safeword," he said. Her hands reached out in front of her, bracing herself on the edge of the couch, her feet dangling helplessly as she laid over his lap. Resting his hand on her bottom, he was pleased to feel how thin the material was beneath his hand. That would do well. He had to ease her into it, and he had no idea what kind of pain tolerance she had.

"I thought you didn't do the lap thing?" she whispered into the couch.

"Up until two minutes ago, you didn't do the submissive thing," he countered. She giggled.

He needed to show her how hot it could be. He wanted her begging him, taken to a place she'd never been before, submitting to his every word, turned on by the loss of control and his power over her.

"What happens to naughty girls, Heidi?" he began in a stern voice. She gasped as she wriggled and he held her in place.

"They get… spanked?" she asked. He lifted his hand and brought it down sharply, not too hard, but firm enough that she no doubt felt the sting.

"That's right," he said, as she squealed from the sting of his hand. He lifted his hand and spanked her again, the crack of his palm echoing through the room. In between spanks he rubbed her bottom and groaned. God, she was so perfect, so full, so fucking gorgeous. He pushed his fingers between her legs and teased her, running a finger firmly over the thin material. She moaned out loud as he found the opening to her top again, and he pinched her hardened nipples. He continued, spanking her firmly but slowly, as he murmured how important it was to obey him and what happened to girls who didn't obey.

She was panting with desire now, fully primed, but her curiosity hadn't yet been sated.

"What would it be like…" she breathed. "Oh God, that's… good, Dom, it's good," she whispered. "But I want to know." He paused as she turned her head to the side. "What would it be like if I were really bad? And you had to punish me? Would it be like that?" she whispered, and he could hear her excitement and nervousness.

Without another thought, he pulled her yoga pants down and bared her to him, holding her firmly. She squealed.

"Did you text in the car tonight?" he asked evenly, voice low, corrective, his hand poised above her vulnerable bottom.

"Um... oh my gosh... yes?" she whispered. He spanked her hard, several stinging swats in succession, with no soft and sensual caressing in between. Her skin reddened beneath his hand as he spanked her again, and again, six sharp, rapid swats that took her breath away.

"Do that again, and this is where you'll be," he promised. His hand fell heavily as he gave her the hardest spank he'd yet given her. She fairly flew off his lap. "You'll not take your safety so lightly."

"Okay!" she said, panting and squirming.

"And if it were a repeated offense?" *Swat! Swat! Swat!* "I'd introduce you to my belt, and the spanking would be even harder."

"Got it!"

He stopped. "You asked, babe," he said, as he pulled her pants up again and released the pressure he had on her lower back. As soon as he did, she was up, up off his lap, and he pulled back in surprise. Was she leaving? Had he pushed her too far? Why was she...

Then her hand was flat against his chest and she shoved him back, straddling him, her mouth on his, and he responded instinctively, his hands flying to tear off her sweatshirt while hers found the edge of his t-shirt. There wasn't enough time, the need was so urgent, he needed her *now* and she was clearly in the same exact position.

He pulled her so that her legs wrapped around him and he stood. She squealed.

"I'm too heavy!"

His only response was a sharp crack to her ass, which made her groan even louder as he stalked to his bedroom and kicked open the door. He tossed her on the bed.

"Take 'em off," he growled as he took a condom out of the drawer next to the bed. She tore her clothes off so quickly he swore he heard something rip. He pushed her gently but firmly down on the bed, lowering himself on her and kissing her, holding her arms above her head and wrapping her legs around him.

"Please," she begged.

He needed no further invitation, but plunged deep within her, her moans ripping through his chest as his own groans mingled with hers, until the final, shattering release of his climax just seconds before hers.

He dropped his head to Heidi's.

They panted in silence for a moment before she spoke again.

"One more question," she panted, as her breathing slowed and he rolled over next to her, pulling her up onto his chest.

"Yeah?" he chuckled.

"Can we do that again sometime?" she whispered, her eyes closed, arm draped over her forehead in total surrender, tucked up against his side.

Chapter 9

Heidi stepped slowly off the elevator and turned left down the elegantly carpeted hallway, deeply conscious of the phone in her pocket, which seemed to be getting heavier and heavier the longer she ignored the unanswered text from Dom.

You left? Where the hell did you go?

A pang of guilt hit her as she trudged toward her office.

Not exactly your finest hour, Heidi, she rebuked herself. *Leaving without an explanation.*

And yet what else was she supposed to have done after she'd found herself tossing and turning all night in Dom's bed? After she had, God help her, asked him, *begged him,* to spank her? After she'd had the best orgasm of her life? After he'd then withdrawn so completely she could practically feel the wall he'd built as if it were a physical thing, and had told her, *ordered her,* to go to sleep in his bed *alone?* If there was an etiquette manual for a situation like this, she hadn't received a copy.

He wanted to know where she'd gone this morning, but the better question was where the hell her brain had gone *last night.*

Stupid, stupid, stupid.

She paused outside the door to her office, her stomach twisting as it always did when she caught the gold lettering on the frosted glass that proclaimed *Heidi Morrow Consulting.* The office wasn't much—just a small reception area and her sparsely decorated office, but it was *hers.* And at least *here* she knew what she was doing.

She could hear Paul on the phone as she opened the door, and silently congratulated herself on not having to get the third-degree, at least until she'd had time to pour herself a cup of coffee and cement her poker-face in place.

"I will give her the message just as soon as she gets in," Paul said into the phone as she shut the door behind her. "Oh, yes, I'm sure she'll be in soon, sir, and she can confirm that herself. Uh huh. Yes. Of course. I know she does, sir."

Heidi smiled to herself as she set her briefcase on the chair by Paul's desk and poured herself a cup of coffee from the machine atop the stacked microwave/refrigerator in the corner that served as their office kitchen. Paul was a godsend. Intelligent, insightful, and unfailingly polite, he could charm the hell out of even the crankiest clients.

He hung up the phone and she turned to look at him.

"That was Reynold Divris from Easterbrook," he began, jotting down a final note on the pad in front of him. "He said it's very urgent that…"

His sentence cut off as he raised his eyes to look at her, finally. He scanned her from head to toe, his eyebrows lifting high, and said, "Holy shit. What happened to you?"

Heidi scowled. There was that intelligent insight. She would have to rethink 'unfailingly polite'.

"What did Mr. Divris want?" she returned, bending over to peer at his notepad.

"He needs to reschedule the meeting for *tomorrow*, Board of Directors is in a tizzy, contracts need to be signed, he can't delay until later in the week," Paul said in a rush, tearing off his notes and handing them to her.

She grabbed the paper and pretended to be consumed with reading it.

"Heidi, I can tell that you've been crying! What…"

"How's Princess? Was she too much trouble this weekend? I'll come pick her up tonight. I can't thank you enough for watching her."

Paul shook his head and said, "It's fine. She's been great. I liked having her. But, Heidi…"

"Tomorrow, huh? I'd better get on this. Thanks, Paul," she said, grabbing her briefcase and her coffee and making a beeline for the relative sanctuary of her office before he could question her further. What she needed was coffee and work, in that order. What she did *not* need was to discuss this, now or *ever*.

But Paul was in her office and closing the door behind him before she could kick it shut.

"I knew this was a bad idea," he scolded her, leaning back against the door, his forehead wrinkled and his pretty blue eyes clouded in worry. "I told you this stuff messes you up!"

Heidi's eyes widened in shock and she momentarily forgot her resolve not to talk.

"You did no such thing! You were the one who was all 'Go for it! It'll be amazing! Doms aren't jerks'!"

She slammed her briefcase down on the desk and whirled to face him, her arms folded across her chest. "Which just goes to show what *you* know."

Paul's head reared back in surprise and a speculative light came into his eyes, one that Heidi didn't like for a second.

"Wait… you were crying about *Dom?*" he asked, straightening. "I thought this was something to do with your *mother*. You know, the woman you were supposed to visit this weekend?"

Oh shit. She'd walked into this one.

"I did visit her. It was… the usual." Heidi shrugged and took the Easterbrook file from her briefcase. "She was busy, so I came home last night instead of waiting until this morning. The drive down was shorter without the Monday morning traffic on 93, you know?" The drive had been shorter because she'd sped the whole way home. Like an idiot.

"Anyway," she went on, not giving him a chance to respond. "I'm going to have to get started on this right away if we have to meet so soon. Have we received the employee information we requested, *finally*?"

Paul shook his head impatiently.

"Not yet. Apparently the board doesn't keep those files, and there's been some hold up getting approval for administration to release the information, with the headmaster being out of the office or something. I'll call Reynold back and see if he can speed things up, but I'm guessing we won't be able to get them until tomorrow at the meeting."

Heidi frowned as she examined the top sheet of the file. Something about this whole situation had been niggling at her.

"You know, I've been thinking about this," she told Paul. "These guys have been epically uncooperative, way beyond the norm for people who need our help to close a budget shortfall. I've thought from the beginning that it seemed shady, but I assumed they were just closing ranks when an outsider came poking around."

Paul nodded. "A reminder that you're just the hired help."

"Exactly." Heidi tapped her finger on the page thoughtfully. "But… now I'm starting to wonder if there's more going on."

Paul raised an eyebrow and leaned his elbows against the table. "Like what?"

"Okay," Heidi said, starting to pace back and forth in the tiny space. "Like… how could a pair of board members make sure that under-qualified students were accepted to the school?"

"I don't know," he said, frowning. "The board has a lot of pull."

"They do, but if getting your kid accepted was as easy as bribing a member of the board, why resort to making fraudulent 'donations' to the school in the first place?"

"Good point. Or an alumnus could just run for a position on the board themselves, and save themselves a ton of money."

Heidi nodded.

"So the process has to be more involved than that. And I'm guessing it involves review and approval from an administrator at the school, right? And, *gosh*, this would all be so much easier if we could get a damn *question* answered!" she finished hotly, rubbing the back of her neck.

"I'm sure I can get that information from Reynold Divris," Paul said. "He might not have the files we need, but he can give us basic information about the acceptance process."

"Okay," Heidi said. "All right. That's a decent first step."

It wouldn't resolve the budget shortfall, but it would clear the way for a better investigation, and it would help keep the school's integrity intact.

"And hound them again about those freaking personnel files, would you? I really want to get them *today*. If the school administration won't cooperate with *you*, maybe they'll cooperate with Mr. Divris if he calls them. Speaking to the person indirectly responsible for your paycheck tends to make people much more agreeable."

Paul snorted.

"But if that doesn't work… I'm just going to have to wing it tomorrow," she told him.

She felt a little thrill of anticipation. Thirty-six full time staff at Easterbrook and she wouldn't know the first thing about any of them before she met them the next day? Yeah, that would pose a challenge, but she'd handled worse before. *This* was her strength.

It was stupid relationship stuff she couldn't handle.

Her phone dinged with a new text and her stomach clenched.

Shit. Ignore it.

She plastered on a smile and held the file out to Paul.

"Can you scan this for me? I'm going to want to review it at home tonight."

He accepted the file with narrowed eyes and a razor blade smile.

"You are *so* cute, thinking I'm going to drop it," he said. "I want to know what happened with Dom. Why were you crying?"

"You know what?" she snapped, throwing her hands in the air as she rounded her desk. "I have had enough with bossy men telling me what to do!"

"Ah," Paul said with a knowing smirk. "Dom's been getting bossy with you? It's tough to get used to at first, honey, but if you like him, you'll learn to go along with it. You might even learn to love it."

"Well, newsflash: I don't like him," Heidi said, yanking out her chair.

"Have you really tried? Because if you do, what you'll get from him will more than make up for…"

Paul cut off as Heidi plopped herself down in the seat and winced at the ache that caused.

"I thought your back was better," he said.

"It is. Much. It's, um… not my back that's sore."

She felt herself blush as Paul's eyes widened in realization.

"Holy shit, Heidi! What happened?"

She wondered if Paul knew that his voice had gotten deeper, was almost a growl now.

With a sigh, Heidi admitted, "Nothing I didn't want to happen at the time, Paul. It's fine."

She sighed as she shifted to a more comfortable position. Then, seeing his thunderous face, she elaborated.

"Okay… It was more than fine… it was… amazing." Mind-blowing, earth-shattering. As though she were a whole different person today than she'd been yesterday... But it was all one-sided, because clearly Dom was looking for another harem member to warm his bed, and she wasn't interested.

Paul's concern faded to confusion as he dropped into his usual folding chair.

"If it was amazing, why were you upset? Did you fuck up badly? Did he punish you hard? If he's got any experience at all, he should know that you're a complete newbie and he needs to use a light hand! Why didn't you safeword?"

Heidi held up a hand against the barrage of questions.

"First of all, no, I didn't 'fuck up'. To fuck up, I'd have to have rules, and I didn't. I don't. I *won't*," she said defiantly. "And second, he only gave me a brief spanking just to... show me what it would be like."

She couldn't meet Paul's gaze and felt her face heating as she continued, "And, you know... one thing led to another."

She darted a quick glance at Paul to see that his eyebrows had climbed again.

"You had sex with him," Paul confirmed.

Heidi gave a small nod.

"You liked the spanking," Paul stated, but Heidi nodded anyway.

"You liked the sex?" This time it *was* a question, and Heidi nodded again.

"So, why the tears?" he asked.

Heidi took a deep breath and bit her lip. She didn't know how to talk about this stuff, not with Paul, not with anyone. She wasn't a prude, but it had somehow always just felt strange to discuss sex—like the very act of discussing it made it seem more important than it was.

Her phone dinged for the third time, and she clenched her hands to prevent herself from reaching for it.

The truth of it was, she wasn't sure how to handle this on her own. She blew out a breath and took a leap of faith.

"So... after the sex, which was, oh, Paul... it was *amazing*," she said, the words erupting in a rush, now that she'd begun.

"That's a good start," he said, settling back in the chair with an encouraging smile. Heidi chuckled weakly.

"I had thought, when I overheard him one time, that he was all cold and detached, you know? Like he was an observer rather than a participant. And I worried that the spanking might feel... humiliating, I guess. But it wasn't like that at all. He was right there with me, the whole time, and I felt... special."

Paul nodded. "Because you are."

Heidi waved this off and continued.

"I made some lame joke, like 'can we do this again?' and he laughed and hugged me tight, and I thought... well, I don't know what I thought. Something very hearts-and-flowers that Hillary would approve of," she confessed, wrapping her hands around her coffee mug.

"But then two seconds later, he practically leaped out of bed like there was a fire! I asked where he was going, and he said he was heading back to work this morning after a week's vacation and he needed his rest, so he was going to sleep." She shook her head, still struggling to understand the abrupt change. "So, okay, I figured we're not ready for sleepovers yet. That's disappointing, but I get it. So, I started to get up, too, and go back to my apartment. But then he gave me this stern look and told me to sleep in his bed while he slept on the couch. No arguments, no explanations, no *affection*. It's like he was two different people from one moment to the next. Trust me to pick the hot guy with multiple personality disorder," she said, with a weak half-laugh.

"Hmmm," Paul said, his eyes narrowed in thought. "What do you know about this guy, Heids? Beyond the fact that he's a dominant?"

"Not much," she admitted. "I don't know what he does for a

living, I don't know what his hobbies are... well, besides... er, you know."

Paul nodded.

"I know he has two brothers. I know he likes dogs and power tools and hamburgers from Roadhouse. I know he goes to a BDSM club, or maybe more than one, and he likes vanilla ice cream and he sends funny texts and he takes safe driving seriously..." she trailed off in a whisper. "Sounds pretty lame, now that I think about it."

God, she couldn't even remember his last name. Had he ever told her?

When had her life become a Carrie Underwood song?

"Sounds like a good beginning, I would have said," Paul disagreed. "The crucial thing here is that you don't know what he wants from you. He goes to a club and... he doesn't do long-term, you said?"

"I've never seen the same girl more than once," she said in a small voice. "Man, I don't know why I let myself get so starry-eyed in the first place! You know that's not like me! It's just..."

And then in a sudden flash of anger, it burst from her, "He *said* he didn't put his submissives over his lap!"

Paul raised an eyebrow.

"He said he didn't do that with *anyone*, that it was really intimate, but he did it with me! He... I guess... somehow... with all the texts and the check-ins and the little lectures about safety... I thought that this was different. That *I* was different."

But it wasn't. And that was her mistake.

Paul's mouth twisted with sympathy.

"Well, if all he wanted was a quick fuck, it was pretty shitty for him to go down that path, especially with someone as inexperienced as you are, without being clear about his expectations. This is *his* fuck-up, Heids, not yours. So, how did Dom the dominant leave things this morning?"

Heidi thought she'd used up all her blushes, but somehow she found one more.

"I... left," she confessed. "Without talking to him. I stayed the night, because I just didn't want to fight about it anymore, but I didn't sleep at *all*. And I couldn't handle any more drama this morning either. So, I waited until he was in the shower and I-I just went home. Then I got all my stuff and showered at the gym."

She saw disapproval in Paul's face, so she quickly explained.

"I just didn't want another argument, Paul! I was feeling really fragile. I have to live next door to this guy, so I know we have to have a conversation eventually, but I wanted it to be later, maybe *much later*, after I've had a chance to get over my stupid disappointment. You know? He made it pretty clear last night that he's all about the bossy and the sex. I was the idiot who turned it into more."

Paul sighed.

"I get that, honey, wanting to protect yourself. But you also didn't give him a chance to explain. You seem to think he's playing you..."

"And you don't?" she interrupted.

"Well... it does seem that way," Paul agreed. "But it also sounds like he was a little confused."

Paul held up a hand when Heidi tried to interrupt.

"He wasn't bullshitting you when he said that it's more intimate to take a submissive over your lap, Heidi. And it's not just intimate for the submissive. It's not just about sparing a sub's feelings or whatever. It's intimate for the dominant, as well."

Heidi rolled her eyes.

"All I'm saying is, don't be so quick to assume that just because Dom's the... well, the *dominant*... that he has all the answers and never has a moment where he's overwhelmed or confused. Maybe this is as new to him, in some ways, as it is to you. If he calls you, talk to him."

Heidi's lips pursed.

"He… maybe… already, um… texted me."

Paul's head jerked.

"And what did he say?"

"I think it was… um… 'where the hell did you go'?" she admitted quietly. "*Shit.*"

"Yeah, 'shit' is about right," Paul agreed.

"And I'm pretty sure he's sent me a couple of other texts too," she whispered. "After that one. I… ignored them."

"Well, then, *triple*-shit, Heidi!" Paul said.

Heidi snickered, despite the anxious feeling that knotted her gut.

"I guess I do owe him a chance to explain, huh? I'll text him back… just as soon as I finish reviewing the Easterbrook file."

Paul laughed out loud.

"Oh, honey! He's texted you *three* times? After he spanked you last night and you walked out on him this morning? And you're gonna review the file *before* you reply? That man has his work cut out for him." Then, with a speculative look at her chair, he added, "You might wanna buy a better cushion."

"What's that supposed to mean?" Heidi asked indignantly.

"If you don't know, you'll find out!" he told her with a wink. He grabbed the Easterbrook file from the table and gestured toward the door. "I'll call Reynold Divris to get the information and confirm for tomorrow morning. Leave this to me. And meanwhile, *you* take care of your other urgent business."

Damn know-it-all. But Heidi sighed and took the phone out of her pocket. Time to figure out how to fix this.

Chapter 10

"I'd spank her," Matteo said, as he replaced the dumbbell back on the rack.

"Big surprise," Dom muttered, arms crossed in front of him, eyes flitting around to see if anyone had heard his brother's casual, but not discreet, announcement. "And why don't you just say it a little louder? I'm not sure the girls over there on the exercise bikes heard you."

Matteo frowned at the weights in front of him and chose a large set of hand weights. He stood in front of the mirror and the tops of his hands hit his thighs before he began pulling up and lifting into bicep curls. The large bulge of his biceps rose as he lifted. Watching his form in the mirror as he spoke, he dropped his voice.

"Like I give a damn about what other people hear or think," Matteo said, his voice strained as he lifted. "And FYI, I don't stand around and shoot shit with guys at the gym, twin brother or not. Grab some fucking weights and let's go."

Dom rolled his eyes and grabbed a set of weights, imitating Matteo's reps.

"You're a pain in the ass," Dom said.

"You're a bigger pain in the ass," Matteo retorted in a sing-song voice.

Dom grunted as he pumped the weights.

"Seriously, man," Matteo said. "She asks you to do what you did. You do. She takes off first thing in the morning for no reason and then doesn't return your messages? Yup. If it were up to me, she wouldn't sit pretty for a week."

Dom didn't disagree. Part of him wanted to do exactly what Matteo said, and if he'd had consent, there would be no question. But he didn't have consent, and he couldn't just go and punish her. It frustrated him to no end that he had no idea *why* she took off on him. He'd called her, texted, and even walked to her apartment, only to pound on a door that went unanswered. Had he freaked her out? She sure as hell hadn't *seemed* freaked out. She'd seemed content, and giddy even, and he thought everything had gone off without a hitch.

Had he fooled himself, thinking that she was somehow different? Had he done what he'd vowed he'd never do, let his guard down and risked everything, taking a chance at more than sexual play, taking her over his *lap* even, revealing the part of him that pulsed with life, like crimson lifeblood in his veins? He'd taken a risk. Had it been a mistake? If it wasn't her thing, couldn't she have at least given him an indication along those lines?

He was also disappointed. He'd felt he'd pleased her, fulfilled desires she likely didn't even know she had, and yet her leaving without a word said otherwise. His mind kept going back to the day before. The unreserved way her head hit the pillow when he'd taken her, and she'd moaned, as she dug her pretty little fingers into his back. He'd felt on top of the world, as Heidi had allowed him to dominate her in the most primal of ways.

And he hated the idea that he'd somehow pushed her away.

The protective side of him feared the worst, that he'd mistak-enly hit a nerve, or scared her, and she'd pulled away from him and left because she was frightened. Was she okay? This wasn't how it was supposed to work. He didn't want to scare her.

He wanted to be the one that made her feel safe.

He pulled himself willfully out of his head and back to the present as he did another curl.

"Consent first," Dom said.

Matteo grunted in return. Consent was a nebulous concept to him. With his charm and luck, he'd land on two feet like a cat every time. But Dom was much more careful, always had been, and his need to stay professional for the sake of his job was crucial.

He glanced at the large clock on the wall.

"Gotta go," he said to Matteo. "Big meeting at work today."

Matteo's raised eyebrows over Dom's shoulders. "Looks like you've got yourself another meeting first."

Dom spun to look, his stomach twisting before he even saw her. He *felt* her.

The first thing that hit him was how beautiful she was, as she walked toward them, her chin held high but her eyes betraying her, fear and uncertainty flickering as she came closer. Her thick mass of hair was held in place with a clip, and she was wearing an outfit that was impossibly sexy for the purpose of sweating. He'd seen those full breasts, the way her cheeks flushed when he'd unleashed the first taste of his authority over her; he'd felt the rapid beating of her pulse against his chest as he'd teased her breasts under the edge of her top. He'd had the pleasure of her over his lap, her warm belly pressed against his thighs.

He'd been under her spell before, and as she neared, he felt the pull again.

But he was the one in charge. And she'd done something she shouldn't have. He had to remain stern, and get to the bottom of this shit before things got even more complicated.

The fact that she hadn't turned tail and run when she caught sight of them meant something.

"Hi," she said weakly. She stood in front of them, one delicate hand on her hip, the other hanging uselessly as if she didn't know what to do with her hands as she spoke.

"Hi," Dom said, and despite his efforts to hold onto his anger, he felt it give way in place of concern. What if she *had* been scared? He hated the thought that he could've done that to her. She needed someone to take care of her, not hurt her. Would she have left if she'd trusted him? A sick feeling twisted in his stomach, and his plans to lecture, scold, and remain aloof fled.

"You okay?" he asked, his voice coming out much softer than he'd planned.

Matteo's eyebrows rose as Dom intentionally ignored him.

Her eyes flicked down to the floor as she nodded. "Yeah," she said.

Matteo looked from one to the other and shook his head. "Well, kids, as much as this engaging conversation has me hooked, I need to pull myself away and get to—"

"Bye," Dom interrupted, with a pointed look at the door.

Matteo waved to Heidi, but as he stood behind her, he mouthed words to Dom, and if the *Spank Her* he mouthed hadn't been exactly clear, the waving motion he made at the air near Heidi's ass sure did. Dom narrowed his eyes and Matteo took off.

Her dangling hand had crossed her belly now, as she held both hands on one hip. She came a bit closer to him, speaking low so they wouldn't be overheard. "We have to talk," she whispered.

He crossed his arms and raised his brows. "You think?" he asked, with deliberate sarcasm. She visibly wilted.

"I'm sorry," she whispered, though it wasn't a repentant sorry. Her eyes had come to his and they were heated, the apology meant to placate. She was pissed herself, it seemed.

"Here isn't the place," he whispered back.

"I know," she hissed, her eyes more clouded now, and as she stepped closer to him, he could smell her, the sweet smell of citrus and spice. She inhaled. "I'm kinda really pissed off at you, though."

"Oh yeah?" he hissed back, taking a step closer, intentionally getting close enough to throw her off her guard. "Because I was the one who left without a word? And didn't return phone calls or texts? After we'd had one fucking awesome time together?"

"You-you… you left, too!" she said, as if the words tumbled out of her mouth before she could speak.

He was so taken by surprise, he felt the anger momentarily pause. "What?"

"Figuratively," she hissed low, and if her accusation hadn't angered him, he'd have grinned at how cute she was. Why did she have to be so cute?

"You just… after I…" To his horror, tears filled her eyes. "I *did* that. Opened myself up like that. Let you—you know—and then we…" her eyes closed shut. "Oh, God." She swallowed hard and her eyes opened up again. "That was the most amazing thing *ever*," she whispered. "And then you just *left* me. Just up and left me, all alone, like you'd had your fill and I was worth nothing." Her voice trembled, and he knew she was trying not to cry. "Just another one of your one-night stands you couldn't even stay in the same room with. How could you *do* that?"

What was she talking about? He thought back on the night she left.

As what she said dawned on him, he was torn between the desire to take her by the shoulders and shake her to make her see sense, and the desire to pick her up in his arms and hold her.

She'd been exhausted. And as she'd curled up against him in bed, he'd felt she needed some rest. He'd told himself if he left her in bed, she could get some sleep, instead of tossing and turning next to him. And he didn't want her to freak out when she woke up in the morning and found she'd slept next to a guy she hardly knew. If she hadn't been so exhausted, he'd have walked her home, but she was so tired, he'd decided he would let her crash in his bed.

It had nothing to do with the fact that he never slept next to the women he took home. It had nothing to do with a reluctance to draw close to her, to ward off any temptation to become intimate in a way he'd avoided successfully for years.

At least that's what he told himself.

"I left you so you could sleep," he explained, and despite his efforts to stay stern and in charge, his voice softened, his reason seeming frail now that he voiced it.

He didn't like the way her lip trembled. He didn't like how she was so far away from him, not when she needed someone to take care of her.

She blinked. "So I could sleep?" she whispered.

He nodded and took a step closer. "Yes," he said, with meaning. God, he'd been so *stupid*. How could he not realize that she'd needed him after she'd been left so vulnerable and exposed? She was a big girl. If she'd wanted to go home, she could've. She hadn't wanted to. She'd wanted to *stay*. "That was stupid of me," he said, overcoming his pride, the desire to make things right with her his only focus. "That was an asshole thing to do, and I shouldn't have done that. I had no idea it would affect you that way, but I shouldn't have been so stupid."

"Oh," she whispered, her eyes leaving his. She spoke to the floor. "And then you messaged me," she said. "And I didn't message you back. And I saw you come and... you knocked on my door," her voice dropping. "I guess that was my stupid move."

He was reluctant to put the blame on her now that he realized how she'd felt, but he also knew that if they were going to pick up where they left off, this kind of breach of trust couldn't be allowed. He'd done his part in apologizing, and he would have to make it up to her.

He had no idea where they were going with this, or what

would happen, but he did know that he wouldn't tolerate what had happened.

"Mmm-hmm," he responded, the stern edge creeping back.

Her eyes went back to his, and now they truly were repentant. "I'm sorry," she whispered, but this time her voice was soft and sincere.

He gave a curt nod, not unaware of the fact that he'd been partly to blame as well. "I am, too," he said. "I had no idea you'd misread my intentions like that."

She exhaled a shaky breath as he took a step closer and reached for her hand. They'd had a misunderstanding and both were at fault. She'd run initially. But she'd come back.

It was time to pick things up where they left off.

Leaving without communicating and then not returning his messages was something that by all intents and purposes, was punishable. He didn't have her consent yet.

But it was time he did.

She was up closer to him now, so close that his breath made the little wisp of a curl next to her cheek move. Her large blue eyes looked up at him, curious but somehow heated, as she whispered, "I should be—are you going to—if it were anyone else, would you…"

"Soundly."

Her breath hitched as she inhaled. She swallowed, and twisted her hand in his as he leaned down and whispered in her ear.

"You left, in the dark, alone," he said. "You put yourself in a dangerous situation. That won't happen again."

"Okay," she whispered.

He leaned closer to her, draping her hair over her shoulder, his fingers lightly touching her neck as he whispered in her ear. "Going forward, the correct response when I reprimand you is 'Yes, sir'."

Her eyes widened and a faint splotch of color rose on each

cheek. "Yes, sir," she whispered, her eyes frantically searching for onlookers who could've heard them, though they were isolated.

He continued to whisper in her ear. "When I called and messaged you, you refused to answer my call or reply. I consider that disrespectful. That alone would earn you a trip over my lap."

She shifted and her eyes shut tight, but she whispered back, "Yes, sir."

Dom had never had real rules for his submissives. They'd always been fabricated rules, as a real expectation of obedience was unnecessary for bedroom play." But it came naturally to him, as he spoke with Heidi. Hell, he'd always been grateful a submissive would be willing to leave with no expectation of anything further. But this was different.

"Heidi," he whispered, and she nodded as she pulled a little closer and he held her a little tighter. "I won't do any of this until we have consent in place. It's not fair to you, and it's not fair to me."

"I consent," she whispered, and he felt a thrill at her words. A small word, a brief conversation, that changed everything. "But there are things I need to know. I feel like we're jumping in with two feet here."

"We are, baby," he whispered, his plans to remain stern softening at the fear he saw in her eyes, the *baby* rolling off his lips before he could think about what he was saying.

"I don't know so much about you! Like… your last name, or what you do for work, or, or… if you like the Red Sox, or where you grew up. How can you… spank me and I don't even know if you like cream or sugar in your coffee?" She blinked rapidly, licking her lips.

He chuckled. She was so damn cute.

"Angelico," he said. "That's my last name. I love the Red Sox… I drink my coffee black." He frowned. "I lost track of everything else."

She giggled and he smiled back. He loved her giggle. It was

so feminine, and he already knew it was a good indication she was at ease now. Suddenly she stiffened in his arms.

"Oh my God, the time," she said. She pulled away from him, her eyes wide on the clock at the wall. He stood himself, the real-ization dawning on him that he was late, too. Shit.

"Tonight," he said, as he pulled away, meeting her eyes as he moved to go. "Tonight, we go over all that stuff. I take you out to dinner. You ask me anything you want, and you get honest answers for everything. You wanna know my high school grade point average, what size underwear I wear, whatever? You ask, I'll answer. But I have to go, too. Six o'clock, my place." He paused. "And we'll deal with what happened," he said sternly, with meaning.

He could tell by the mix of nervousness and excitement that crossed her face that she knew exactly what he meant.

Though he'd stated his purpose, he raised an eyebrow to check to see if she was cool with that.

"I'll be there," she said. She paused. "And… okay." Her voice dropped. "Yes, sir." She turned and fled.

Damn. He had thirty minutes to shower and get to work. He'd never once been late for work.

He trotted to the locker room lightly, ready to turbo shower and head in.

She mesmerized him.

She'd forgiven him.

He'd look forward to tonight.

———

It took a concentrated effort to focus on the task at hand, as he pulled the nose of his red Toyota into place, his eyes momentarily resting on the sturdy sign in front of his parking space *Reserved for Headmaster Mr. Angelico,* next to the sign marked *Reserved for Mr. Divris.* There were only two assigned spaces, Headmaster and

Head of Board of Directors. Seeing the assigned space next to his reminded Dom of the impending finance meeting, which he'd intentionally put out of his mind during his week-long vacation. He sighed. Back to the grind.

Despite the fact that they both were rushing to work, Heidi had managed to message him several times, and he'd responded each time. She'd been flirty, and responded to each of his own texts. She was witty, and he loved that the tension had fled between them. He had every intention of giving her the time of her life tonight. She could ask her questions, as he dined her, and they could establish the trust he knew they needed. He knew he would have to spank her, and he pushed away the heat he felt pool in his stomach at the thought of taking her over his lap again. It was hard to really punish her, but he could get his point across quite well without being overly harsh. She didn't need harsh. She was new to this, and they'd both been at fault. She *did* need to know he meant what he said.

He picked up his laptop bag and slung it over his shoulder, as he shut the door and headed for the entrance.

"Hi, Mr. Angelico!" came a high-pitched voice behind him. He turned, raising a hand in salute to the flock of students that crowded the entrance of the school. He wasn't sure who'd addressed him, but greeted them en masse.

He could not think of Heidi, and he certainly couldn't think of Heidi over his lap, now. Now, he had work to do. Now, he had to focus on the job at hand.

He continued to text her as he made his way to the office.

I have a meeting shortly, he'd messaged. *You being a good girl?*

Shoving his phone in his pocket as he entered the hallway, students milling about him, instinctively he was on alert, the headmaster in charge, looking to feel the pulse of his students, eyes scanning for anything awry, but everything looked kosher. He nodded, occasionally gracing them with a brief smile, fully aware that students stood straighter and spoke more quietly as he walked past them to his office. He was aware of the presence he held, and he did his best to maintain that presence. That air of authority was one way he was able to maintain the order and decorum he did.

His phone buzzed at the same moment the first bell rang, and students scattered. He waited until he was in the safe confines of his private office to glance at her reply text.

I'm always a good girl.

He smiled.

That could get boring.

Her reply was almost instantaneous. *I'll keep that in mind.*

He chuckled. *I've got to run and won't be available until later. Looking forward to tonight. I'll message you at lunch.*

I have to go, too. About to drive and putting my phone down.

Good girl.

He'd used that simple phrase—*good girl*—just a few times with her, but every time he could see the pleasure it brought her.

"Some girls will take offense to 'good girl'," Matteo had once said, as they sat at The Club, pulling at beers in their hands, eyes on the crowd. "They get all pissy and think it's an insult. But a submissive girl, she'll love it. It's a good sign, before you even get to anything else. She melts when you call her your good girl, she's got a submissive inside, even if she's still lurking."

He put his phone on the edge of his desk, face down, as he arranged the papers he'd need and steeled himself for the upcoming meeting. A small voice nagged at the back of his mind, reminding him how essential it was to separate his work from his private life. Heidi's obedience and submission to him made him feel ten feet tall. But even then, even though it was a positive, motivating sense of doing what he was meant to do, he felt it was dangerous to allow the high he'd gotten from making up with her, and the promise of an exciting evening up ahead, to color the work ahead of him. With a will, he focused on what he had to do.

Where had the folder he needed gone to? He'd had a meeting right before vacation with the business manager, and all his papers had been neatly arranged in preparation for the meeting today. He'd been fanatical about it, even, because he wanted this meeting to go off without a hitch. And now, the blue folder he'd placed right on top of those papers was nowhere to be seen. Picking up the phone on his desk, he dialed his secretary.

"Good morning, Mr. Angelico," Louisa said pleasantly on the other line.

"Morning, Louisa," he said, feeling the impatience of the necessary pleasantries. "I have an important meeting in a few minutes and can't seem to locate a crucial folder. Have you seen a blue folder that I left on my desk before vacation?"

"No, sir, I haven't been in your office, and don't recall seeing a folder. But I'll look through what I have here anyway, in case it somehow mistakenly ended up with my papers." Louisa was fastidious, stringently tidy, and an accidental paperwork mistake seem unfathomable. He sighed.

"Thank you," he said. "And please let me know when the consultants we've hired have arrived."

"They've already arrived, sir," she said, and at the same time, he heard a knock on his office door.

"Thank you, Louisa," he said, as he hung up the phone. "Come in."

Jay Divris, the head of finance at the school, entered. He was the son of Reynold Divris, head of the Board of Directors, and was to the school what old money was to a town—alumni, born and raised to be Easterbrook material. He was always poised and on his game, but today he looked stricken. Tall, thin, and wiry, he moved quickly and with purpose. He ran a hand through his tuft of thinning dark hair, and adjusted his wire-rimmed glasses on his nose.

"Dom," he said in greeting, with a curt nod. Dom nodded in return.

"Good vacation?"

"Relaxing," Dom said, moving immediately past small talk, as he could tell Jay was bothered by something. "Everything okay?"

"The Board of Directors insisted on meeting with the consultants before we did," he said in a rush, sitting heavily at the chair on the opposite side of Dom's desk. It seemed everyone who sat in that chair was always on edge, emotionally-charged, or near tears. Students who faced suspension or expulsion, weepy mothers who feared for the disciplinary actions against students who'd broken school rules, teachers who were stressed or angered, or feared a pending layoff. He did what he always did. He took a calming breath, folded his hands atop his desk, and nodded to Jay.

"A reasonable request," he said. "Though you know I'd love to be a fly on the wall in there; it seems if we all move forward with the same end-goal in mind, we should be able to find common ground. No?"

Jay gave another nod. "I agree," he said. "Though it disturbs me that the financial paperwork I had prepared for today's meeting has gone missing."

Dom was immediately on edge. "You overheard my conversation with Louisa?" he asked, confused.

Jay gave him an equally-confused look. "Louisa? No. I was talking about the quarterly reports I left on my desk." He eyed the closed door behind him. Satisfied it was shut tight, he leaned forward, elbows on his knees, as his voice dropped. "It should come as no surprise that I trust you," he said.

Dom nodded, pleased, but curious what Jay's point was. Jay continued.

"What bothers me is that I can't trust everyone here," he said. Despite the relative warmth of the room, Dom felt a chill come over him. Up until recently, he had, like nearly everyone else on the staff, assumed that the funds that had been inappropriately obtained by the two former board members had been an isolated incident. Though they'd investigated, no one on staff had been implicated in the affair.

"Go on," Dom said. Jay's voice dropped even lower.

"I was contacted by the consultant group we're meeting with this afternoon, and asked to provide the necessary paperwork. I faxed it to them, then intentionally left the papers in a folder on my desk."

"I did the same," Dom said, his hackles rising as he suspected where this story was going.

"Yours still here?" Jay asked.

Dom sat back in his chair, placing his fingertips together.

"Nope."

Jay's eyes narrowed.

"Yet whoever the fool was who took them didn't realize that a paper trail is easily copied," he said. He leaned back and crossed his arms across his chest. "I have everything saved on the server and to a flash drive I took home with me."

Dom smiled wryly. "Good move," he said. "Though I don't like the fact that, clearly, we have underhandedness going on."

"Me neither," Jay said grimly. A knock came at the door, and both men sat up straighter.

"Come in," Dom called, and the door opened. An older woman, with short, curly gray hair, thick glasses and a small, snub nose, peeked in.

"Mr. Angelico, the conference room is prepared for your meeting, but I've not yet found your folder," she said. "It's vacant, but I've put out refreshments and everything else you requested."

"Thank you, Louisa," Dom said, standing and pulling his suit coat from the back of his chair, quickly slipping it on. "Mr. Divris and I have the paperwork covered, but I do thank you for looking."

Louisa gave a polite nod. "Would you like me to fetch anything else for the meeting?"

"No, thank you," he said, gesturing for Jay to join him as he exited his office and headed for the conference room.

"You said the consultants are meeting with the Board of Directors first?" Dom asked, walking so briskly Jay fairly trotted to keep up with him.

"Yes," he said. "They're due to join us in about fifteen minutes."

"Good," Dom said. "That will give us a chance to discuss what we hope this consultation can achieve." Dom was grateful they'd be the first ones in the room, as he felt being the first there would give him an upper hand. It burned to think that someone on his very staff was untrustworthy.

The room to the conference room was ajar, and he pushed it open as Jay continued. "I heard the woman who runs this show is a bit of a ball-buster," he said. "My wife's best friend had a run-in with her a month ago in town, and on her recommendation, she sent a quarter of the staff packing. Said lay-offs, or the company folds."

"Great," Dom said, "If these people think they're going to come in here and layoff my staff, I—" he began to say, but as he pushed the door open, the words froze on his lips.

The conference room was *not* vacant. The consultants were no longer meeting with the Board of Directors.

Sitting at the table was one very handsome, very well-dressed, stranger Dom knew immediately to be on the consultant team who'd been called in to help set the books to rights. The look on his face was placid, but barely pleasant, and Dom knew without a doubt that he'd overheard the last bit of conversation he and Jay had had before they'd entered the room. But it wasn't the well-dressed stranger who held his attention. Next to him, wide-eyed, with flushed cheeks, her hands clasped so tightly atop the table her knuckles were white, sat Heidi.

Chapter 11

Not possible.

She'd repeated those words to herself a dozen times in the minute that had passed since she'd first heard his distinctive smoky voice from the doorway, even checking her phone—which she'd deliberately placed face-down and slightly out of reach on the conference room table to prevent herself from obsessively checking for new texts while in her meeting—to see if she'd somehow, impossibly, managed to call him just by thinking his name. But, no, Dom's scowl was too fierce for her to have imagined, so apparently, it *was* possible. Dom was *here*, and he was furious.

She felt Paul shift in his seat and could sense him watching her, expecting her to rise and get the situation under control, to do her *job* and diffuse the instant tension that had gripped the room, but she was trapped, unable to turn her gaze away from Dom's.

"Good morning," Paul said, breaking the silence by rising to his feet smoothly and extending his hand. "I'm Paul Lozano. And you're Mr.... Angelico?"

"Call me Dom," he replied, gripping Paul's hand, though his eyes never left Heidi's.

Heidi's own hands felt like blocks of ice, as all of the available blood in her body had rushed to her cheeks, stealing her breath and leaving her unable to do more than stare at Dom's face in horror. Just a few hours ago, those jade green eyes had felt like salvation. She'd been his 'baby', his 'good girl'. But now…

A ball-buster… that's what the other man had called her. It wasn't the first time she'd heard that, of course. She'd definitely been called worse. Suggesting layoffs as one possible way to cut costs was part of her job, and she made a convenient scapegoat for employers who wanted to take the quickest path out of bankruptcy. She thought she'd developed a thick skin over the years, but today, knowing Dom had heard it, seeing the hostility in his eyes… Shit, but it stung.

She heard Paul inhale sharply as he recognized Dom's name, and her face flushed impossibly hotter even as part of her wanted to laugh. *Yeah, Paul, this is the guy.*

"Uh… Jay Divris," the other man volunteered, when it appeared that no one was going to introduce him, and Dom's magnetic gaze finally shifted and freed her.

She felt a quick pulse of sorrow in her belly. Things had seemed so damn promising a few hours ago. She felt a momentary desire to just sit back down and follow Dom's lead, let him sort the whole mess out.

And it was that impulse that finally launched her to her feet. She hadn't gotten where she was by being sweet and submissive with her clients, and if that was the type of girl Dom needed, well… better to know that now.

She took a deep breath and extended her own hand.

"Heidi Morrow," she told Jay Divris with a firm handshake. "Why don't we sit down, gentlemen?"

As the men took their seats and shuffled their papers, Paul reached out and laid his hand on Heidi's wrist in a questioning gesture, an unspoken *Are you okay?* Heidi gave him a brief half-smile, and was surprised to see Paul's lips quirk in amusement. What the hell was funny?

Paul glanced pointedly across the table, and Heidi lifted her gaze to find Dom staring fixedly at Paul's hand on her wrist.

Without conscious thought, she pulled her wrist away from Paul and took her own seat.

"Ms. Morrow, Mr. Lozano," Jay began in a placating tone, almost before everyone had taken their seats. "I'm sorry for the conversation you overheard as we were walking in. It was very unprofessional."

Well, wasn't that an interesting opener? Heidi saw her surprise mirrored on Dom's face and felt like giggling. Clearly Dom didn't feel that he owed anyone an apology at all, the jerk.

As though he felt her looking at him, his expression blanked and he sat back in his seat with his arms folded.

She almost forgave Jay for his ball-buster comment. Almost. But then…

"But you have to know why we're a bit on-edge. I mean, your reputation *is* fairly well-known," he concluded, tossing Dom a smirk that said exactly what he thought of that reputation. "I think if we're going to start off on the right foot, we need to set some ground rules…"

Heidi gritted her teeth.

"Mr. Divris," she interrupted sweetly. "I've earned a reputation for helping clients find a path to fiscal solvency. Often, the path they choose requires hard choices. But those are not *my* choices. And since we…"

"You make them fire people!" Jay interrupted.

"Of course we don't," Paul returned calmly. "We don't have the authority to do that, for one thing."

Jay harrumphed.

"That's absolutely accurate," Heidi agreed. "We make recommendations. That's all. And, frankly…"

"That must be tough," Dom challenged, eyes focused some-where behind her head.

These were the only words he'd spoken, besides his name, and they instantly captured everyone's attention.

"*What* must be tough?" Heidi clenched her hands under the table and struggled to keep her emotions in check. Some rational part of her brain knew that she'd lost control of this meeting—if she'd ever had it to begin with—and she needed to focus. But how could she when just hearing his voice, seeing his distant expression, wreaked havoc on her emotions?

"Working under someone else's authority," he explained, his green gaze meeting hers squarely.

Did Dom really just say that?

The sudden tension in Paul's body confirmed that indeed, he had.

"I imagine it would be much easier to just make all of your own decisions and keep all of your *information* to *yourself*, wouldn't it?" he mused.

Jay seemed ready to high-five him in thanks for his support.

Heidi's heart began to pound. Oh, no. He would *not* put this on her. Keeping her information to herself? When *she* had been the one to demand a reckoning and *he* had been the one to put it off?

Her temper flared.

"Not at all, Mr.... I'm so sorry, *what* was your name again?" she pretended to scan the sheaf of papers in front of her.

"Dom."

A single word, spoken in a tone ringing with authority. Not just his name, but his essence. A happy accident when his mother filled out his birth certificate. Dom.

She inhaled sharply, and felt her anger evaporate. She spoke the truth as clearly as she could.

"I have no problem submitting to authority when that authority is clearly defined—when everyone's *roles* are clearly defined. I've been authorized to do a specific job, Dom. I'm going to do it."

There was no challenge in her statement, just a plea for understanding.

He nodded once, an acceptance, before looking away.

But God, what did that mean? Accepting that she needed to do this job, and that it was separate from what they shared? Or accepting that this was... the end?

She was angry with both of them suddenly. Why did it have to be the end? They were both mature adults. And she wanted this, wanted *him*, more than she could ever remember wanting anything.

"I can't make anyone do anything they don't want to do," she said softly, looking around the table, but speaking only to him. "I honestly don't want to. The final decision is yours. If anyone is going to lose their—position—it will be your decision, not mine."

Dom's eyes lifted to hers and held. She could see hope and caution warring in them.

"That's ridiculous!" Jay banged his fist on the table, commanding their attention and interrupting the moment. "My father and the *board* make those decisions, not us. And *you* give your recommendations to the board! Dom and I are the only ones at this table without any say in this process."

"Not true," Paul interjected, before Heidi could speak. He speared Jay with a hostile look. "We make many recommendations and propose several different solutions—that's what we're hired to do. But our recommendations are only as complete as the information you provide to us, which, thus far, has been almost *nothing.* Our goal is to work *together* with you, cooperatively, but in order to do that, you need to provide us with the information we've requested. If you can propose additional sources of revenue or budget cuts, we would be happy—no, *thrilled!*—to present those possible solutions to the board. Believe me, no one wants to see anyone lose a job over this, least of all Ms. Morrow and I."

Jay shook his head incredulously. "If there were additional sources of revenue, don't you think we'd have tapped them? If there were padding in the budget, don't you think we would have cut it?" he demanded. He looked to Dom for support, but Dom's eyes were fixed on Heidi.

"What I *think*," Heidi replied, "is that we are well-versed in looking for unusual sources of revenue, and uncommon ways of trimming budgets. Every situation is unique, Mr. Divris. What I *hope* is that we can work together to figure out solutions that will work for us in *this particular* situation."

Damn. Was she clear enough? Did Dom understand what she was trying to tell him? She shifted her gaze to his.

He understood.

He unclenched his arms and sat forward, hands on the table.

"What I *know*," he said, echoing Heidi's words, "And I think you'll agree, Jay, is that we have an untenable situation here."

Dom looked at Heidi speculatively. She nodded. They couldn't go on this way.

Jay reluctantly nodded too, though Dom didn't even glance in his direction.

"Trust is the key," Dom continued. "And right now there seems to be a lack of trust between us… I mean, between us and certain members of the *board*."

Jay snickered. "They act like we need babysitters. Which is pretty ironic, considering *they* are the ones who fucked the whole thing up."

Dom raised an eyebrow at Jay's language. So much for Jay's professionalism.

"*Anyway*," Dom continued, with another significant glance at Heidi. "It's difficult to have a relationship with the board, since they insist on *withholding information* from us. We didn't even know that they'd hired an independent consultant until last week."

Back to the whole withholding information thing? No way, buddy. That won't fly.

"Is that entirely the board's fault?" Heidi interjected smartly. "Seems as though information was withheld on *both sides*."

And that was true not only of her relationship with Dom, but of the information Easterbrook had withheld from Heidi.

"We just learned from Mr. Divris this morning that there must have been someone on staff—a member of the in-house review board—who approved these unqualified applications. And that you conducted an internal investigation, but that staff member has never been caught or disciplined. Trust is a two-way street."

Dom raised his chin to acknowledge her point and pursed his lips thoughtfully, though his eyes twinkled.

"I appreciate your desire to have the culprit caught and *disciplined*, Ms. Morrow. I think we'll work together very well."

This time it was Paul who smothered a laugh. Heidi was too busy squirming in her seat, gripped by an acute wave of lust brought on by the one-two punch of his words and the deep, smoky voice in which he said them. How had the entire table not caught on fire?

Jay sighed, clearly unable to read the particular variety of tension that charged the air, but understanding that Dom was no longer on his side.

"So," Dom continued softly, no doubt confirming Jay's fears. "While we might wish that this situation were different, we've got to solve this problem together. We will trust you to fulfill your role, and you can trust us to help you with whatever you need."

Heidi drew a sharp breath and stared at him.

Work together. Like partners. Equals. With clearly defined roles and authority.

"That sounds," she began, her voice abnormally husky. She cleared her throat and tried again. "That sounds perfect."

Dom nodded and one side of his mouth quirked up in a smile. "Yeah."

Paul cleared his throat meaningfully, recalling them to their surroundings, and Heidi dropped her gaze to her papers, rubbing a hand over her stinging nose.

"You're confident it can be solved?" she forced herself to ask.

"I am." No doubt whatsoever.

"Just that easy?" she challenged, smiling at him.

"Not easy," he argued, and she could hear the unspoken *baby* in the tender tone he used. "But with trust and effort all around? Hell yes."

Heidi nodded. As their voices continued to buzz around her, discussing the various reviews that would need to be conducted, she closed her eyes tightly. The wall that separated her professional mask from her churning emotions was crumbling and she needed a moment to shore it up.

"Ah, dang it!" Paul said loudly, and her eyes flew open. "*Jeepers*! I am such an *idiot*! I forgot my printout of the salary projections for next year! Must've left them on my desk!"

Heidi shook her head in confusion. *Jeepers?* Since when did Paul talk like a refugee from *Leave it to Beaver?* Plus, the salary projections were right there in the packet he'd prepared for her. She'd seen them just moments before.

"But, Paul, they're right…"

She grabbed her packet and began leafing through it, but Paul snatched the papers from her hands with a firm shake of his head.

"Nope. Sorry, Heidi, but I forgot to put them in *both* of our packets. *Darn!*"

He lifted woebegone eyes to Jay and gave an exaggerated gasp.

"Oh, but wait! Mr. Divris, *you* sent me those projections in the first place! Why, I bet you could print out another copy for us to review!"

"Uh…" Jay seemed taken aback by this strange display of emotion, and glanced around the table for help, but Heidi was as confused as he by her assistant's sudden personality transplant, and Dom… well, Dom just looked amused.

"I guess so," Jay allowed.

"Perfect!" Paul enthused, grabbing up all of his papers as well as Heidi's, and shoving them in his briefcase. "So why don't you and I go ahead and review those papers, Mr. Divris? Maybe in your office? And Heidi, you can go ahead and do the tour, and I'll meet you back at the office later this afternoon."

"The… the tour?" Heidi asked, as understanding began to dawn.

"I'd be happy to show you around the building, Ms. Morrow," Dom offered, his green eyes searing into hers. "Maybe discuss our respective opinions on things over lunch, as a gesture of good will?"

Heidi swallowed. "Oh! Of course. Yes. Definitely. A tour."

"Right," Dom said, rising to his feet. "Shall we?"

He held out his hand to her and gestured to the door. She practically leaped from her seat.

"Follow me, Miss Morrow?" he asked, as he pushed open the door.

"Yes," she said breathlessly. "I will."

Paul winked at her as she passed him.

"Alrighty, then! Meeting adjourned!"

The early-afternoon sunlight made a dappled pattern on the pavement as Dom swung his car into the nearly-empty lot in front of their buildings and screeched to a halt under a large oak tree.

She hadn't touched him at all during the twenty-minute ride home from the school, nor had they spoken since leaving the conference room. He'd walked down the school corridors without pausing, until they reached the back door of the school—the door closest to the parking lot, she learned. He'd held the door open, ushered her through, and steered her directly toward his car—parked in the headmaster's spot, she'd noticed. He'd opened her door, watched her swing her legs inside, and seemed to be on the verge of saying something... but he hadn't. The tension, the *wanting*, between them was absolutely combustible, and both of them seemed to understand that a single word or casual touch would set it off. Instead, he'd buckled himself into the driver's seat and she'd focused on the road, trying to hurry the car along by the force of her mind, as though the brutal pace Dom set (so much for *him* obeying posted speed limits! Ha!) wasn't enough. Anticipation bubbled in her veins, a sparkling eagerness and expectation that left her lightheaded. She was drunk on desire.

Still, once Dom had shifted the gear to *Park* and cut the engine, neither of them moved. The air between her arm and his fairly sparked with electricity, but neither of them acknowledged it, nor said a word. Now that they were here, the reality of what was about to happen, the import of it, seemed to hit them, and Heidi wasn't sure what to do next.

They were together now, that much was clear, if not from their stilted, innuendo-laden conversation around the conference table, then by their unceremonious escape from the school. And they would work together to define terms for their relationship, both inside and outside of school. But... what would that look like? What would the terms be? They needed to discuss all of this before...

Dom turned to look at her, and the heat radiating from eyes seared all the rational thought from her brain.

In an instant, she was fumbling for the door handle with both hands and running up the tree-lined path to her building, with

Dom so close behind that she could feel his harsh breaths on the back of her neck.

She ran faster.

"Keys," Dom demanded, and just that single word made her tremble violently.

Shit! Where were her keys? In her purse, which she'd just left in the...

"Back in the car!" she moaned.

Without breaking stride, Dom swung right, towards his building. He quickly unlocked the door and Heidi stumbled through it, into the cool silence of his entryway.

Before she could draw breath, Dom was in front of her, pushing her back against the door, his body flush against hers, his lips on her throat.

Her arms rose to touch him, but he grabbed both of her wrists in his hands and pinned them to the door above her head.

"Once we start, Heidi, I'm not gonna stop," he told her, and she wasn't sure if it was a threat or a vow, but either way her answer was the same.

"Yesss," she breathed.

His tongue darted out to lick the sensitive spot just below her ear, a gesture of approval for her quick agreement, and Heidi felt her knees buckle as sensation overwhelmed her. Everything about him excited her—the sight of the broad shoulders beneath his dark blue suit jacket, the strong but gentle hold of his fingers on her wrist, the spicy smell of his aftershave, and the raspy arousal of his voice as he spoke to her.

"I don't know if you understood what you agreed to, back in that conference room, what you *gave me*, but here's our new agreement. You don't like something, you don't understand something, you're freaked out about something, you talk to me, and we will find a solution."

The steam of his breath against her throat made it nearly impossible to concentrate on his words.

"Right," she whispered, shifting her head to allow him better access.

"And," he said, pausing to grasp her earlobe with his teeth and make her gasp. "You do whatever you need to do when you're out there. You built yourself a career you're proud of. I would never want this, *us*, to fuck that up. But in here, Heidi…"

His voice descended to a growl.

"In here, you belong to me."

As he spoke the words, he pressed his hips more firmly into hers, and she could feel the hard length of his erection burning against her stomach, marking her.

She closed her eyes.

"God, yes," she whispered drunkenly.

And then suddenly he was gone.

Her eyes flew open. In the bright sunlight that flooded the entryway from the sidelights to the left and right of the door, she saw him standing several steps away, hands fisted at his sides, eyes fixed on her face, chest heaving beneath his fitted dress shirt.

"Shirt first, Heidi," he commanded, his voice raw. "Nice and slow."

"Sh… shirt?" She could hear the dreamy quality of her own voice, the sound dampened by the thrum of blood in her ears.

"Show me, baby," he murmured.

She licked her suddenly dry lips.

He wanted her to strip for him?

Good. Lord.

She could feel a pulse low in her belly.

Eyes on his, Heidi lifted her hands to the top button of her shirt and took a step toward the hall that led to his bedroom.

He moved a single step to block her path.

"Right here, Heidi."

Here? In the bright sunlight coming from the frosted glass windows?

As though he could read the questions in her mind, he repeated, "Right. Here. Right. Now."

He slowly shrugged off his suit jacket and tie, then leaned against the wall and folded his arms, watching her.

If he had looked the slightest bit disinterested or aloof, if his voice had held even the slightest hint of the detachment he'd shown his other ladies, she couldn't have done it. But his eyes didn't so much as flicker away from her hands as they carefully slid down the placket of her blouse, freeing each button from its buttonhole. And the tension that gripped his body belied his casual pose, as did the massive erection tenting the front of his pants.

Mr. Angelico wasn't disinterested. Not at all.

When all of the buttons were opened, she shrugged and let the thin material fall to the floor. She looked at him expectantly, waiting for his next instruction.

"The camisole," he rasped.

Heidi was suddenly breathless.

Crossing her arms in front of her stomach, she slid the edge of the silky material from beneath her skirt and slipped it up, up, up. Each inch of her belly heated as she exposed it, warmed by the blazing heat in his eyes. It glided softly over her skin, raising goose bumps, tightening her nipples to hard peaks, until she lifted her arms completely and let the material fall to the floor with a soft *whoosh*.

"Christ." It was a whisper, a harsh release of breath.

Dom was breathing hard now—she could see his chest rising and falling, could almost feel the force of will required to hold him in place. Her own need was a savage thing—a clawing in her stomach stronger than anything she'd ever felt before. Still, she stood and waited for his next command.

"Skirt," he barked, his eyes holding hers for a single blistering instant, before returning to watch her fingers work.

Standing half-naked, following orders from a man who was

fully dressed and thoroughly aroused, so eager to see her naked he hadn't bothered to take the short trip to the bedroom yet, Heidi had never felt more powerful in her entire life. Every molecule of Dom's focus, his every thought and every desire at this moment were concentrated on her, and she freakin' loved it. There was no room for doubt or embarrassment when he looked at her that way.

Heidi braced her heels further apart and reached for the closure of her skirt. The zipper made a scratching sound as she slowly, slowly slid it down, and she could practically feel his anticipation as he waited for the skirt to fall. She hesitated a moment, deliberately holding the fabric in place, waiting for him to notice and make eye contact, thrilled when he did. With a slow smile, she let the fabric go, and felt it pool at her feet.

"Panties… slowly."

His command had arousal spiraling in her belly, made her head light and her knees weak. Hooking her fingers into the waistband, she slowly peeled the last garment she wore down her body. Once the silk had reached her ankles, she stepped out and tossed the panties aside. With knees shaking harder, she reached a hand behind her to brace herself against the door, and waited for him to speak.

But he seemed to have lost the ability.

He was vibrating with tension, his hands splayed out on the wall behind him in an effort to hold himself back. She waited breathlessly for him to regain control.

She saw the moment he decided to abandon this game. With a harsh indrawn breath, he took a deliberate step toward her, and then another, like an animal hunting its prey—a man pushed to the limits of civility by arousal.

His hands skimmed slowly up her hip to palm her breasts, then further around to her back… then suddenly spun her around so her nipples pressed against the shockingly cold door.

"Are you my good girl?" he demanded, his hands skimming up her sides to collect her wrists and pin them to her lower back.

"Yes," she whispered without hesitation, her body pliant as she rested her cheek against the cool wood.

"But you misbehaved, Heidi," he said severely.

"But I thought… I thought we would work everything out? I thought we agreed…" Her thoughts had scattered like the dust motes spiraling through the air.

"That was later. This morning, Heidi," he reminded her, his voice a heated whisper in her ear. "You said you'd consent to punishment. You agreed."

Heidi moaned. She needed him to touch her. She needed him to kiss her. She needed…

"Heidi," he whispered, tugging her hair in way that was too firm to be playful. That tug seemed to free her from her stupor, while it resonated all the way to her womb.

"Yes," she moaned. "Yes, I agreed."

And she did. She wanted that punishment. She wanted his focus and his control and his need. She wanted *him*.

The first slap of his hand on her bottom was a shock. The second seemed to light a fuse connected directly to her clit. The third… the third had her pushing back against him, waiting for it eagerly. And then his hand was no longer spanking her, but rubbing her bottom with slow strokes that went lower and lower and built the fire into a conflagration.

"Oh, Dom, *please*," she begged, beyond caring how desperate she sounded.

"You won't walk away again," he crooned, pressing his erection against her stinging backside. "You'll never fail to answer a text from me again."

She shook her head wildly.

"Say it!" he demanded.

"I will… never, *never* run away again. I will… oh… I will *never* fail to answer a text!" she sobbed.

"*That*'s my good girl," he approved, reaching around to pinch her hardened nipples in a way that made her lean her head back against his shoulder for support. "Fuck, Heidi. You're so sweet."

His tongue drew circles on her neck, making her crazy, while his hands skimmed down her front to tease her unmercifully.

"Shit, I can't wait. Baby, you make me lose my mind," he whispered. He positioned her compliant limbs in exactly the position he wanted them, bracing her arms against the door. She heard the hiss of his zipper, the rip of a condom packet, and then, before she had time to form a conscious thought, he was inside her so deep, *so damn deep.*

He paused for a moment like that, letting them both adjust.

"This is it, Heidi. There'll never be anything as sweet as this," he slurred. And somehow, knowing that he was as lost to this as she was, ratcheted her need even higher.

"Nothing. Ever," she breathed, knowing it was true. He began to move, fusing them together so that she couldn't tell where she ended and he began. And when the world exploded a moment later, she couldn't tell if the harsh cry echoing in the hallway was his or hers.

Chapter 12

Dom took in the view he'd never tire of watching—Heidi sitting at his kitchen table, legs tucked under her, checking her e-mail on her phone. She'd already been up early, ran to her apartment to take her dog out for a walk, and she came back.

She'd come back.

The fact that she looked totally normal and natural sitting at his kitchen table was not lost on him.

"Gotta check in with Paul," she murmured, and he had a quick, involuntary flex of jealousy at the sound of a male name coming from her lips, a guy she had to 'check in with'. She looked up at him. "My assistant," she said, growing sheepish. He felt sheepish himself.

Grunting in response, he chided himself for being all jealous and stupid over her co-worker. Of course, the guy's name was Paul. He'd met him just yesterday. He knew they had to have the talk, but he'd hoped it would be after he'd had his coffee.

He had to get his shit together. Never for a minute had he suspected she'd be working for the consulting company. There was a time when he'd have been more aware of details, but he'd slipped as of late, distracted by Heidi and all that had happened so quickly. He'd taken her home and gotten right down to it, what they both really wanted, what they both really yearned for. He hadn't been able to bring himself to give her a hard spanking —they were too new, and he could make his point clear without being too hard on her. He'd ease her into his expectations.

They'd *both* ease into it.

They'd made love, and when she'd brought up the work fiasco, he'd told her they'd talk about it in the morning, and to get some sleep. No, he'd *commanded* it. But she'd obeyed.

He'd needed some time to think it through.

They'd both risen before the sun rose, and she'd scooted over to her apartment while he got the coffee. Now was as good a time as any.

He looked out his kitchen window, seeing the sun rise low over the pine trees in the back of his building. He'd always loved this apartment view. No blacktop behind the kitchen, but a yard filled with dappled maples and sturdy pines. The leaves on the maples and oaks had just begun to fill in, and the stark contrast of naked branches against sky was beginning to blur.

He could feel her eyes on him as he stared out the window. He needed to show her this was going to work out.

He needed to show her he was in charge.

She needed it.

He needed it.

"Cream?" he asked. She nodded. "Sugar?" She nodded again. He handed it to her, watching as she poured cream and a dash of sugar into her cup. She stirred, lifted the cup to her lips, and sighed at the first sip.

"This is awesome," she murmured, and he wasn't sure if she was talking about the coffee, sitting in his kitchen, or the whole package.

Taking a seat across from her, he lifted his mug to his lips and took a long pull, feeling the hot, bitter liquid course down his throat. He took another swig, feeling ready to take on what he had to face this morning.

Workplace dynamics and potential wrinkles.

Setting ground rules with Heidi.

Introducing her to the dark, erotic lifestyle it was his pleasure to reveal to her. He thought of the night before, how she'd squirmed and moaned, then screamed in ecstasy.

How much did she want? How much did she *need*?

"What are you thinking?" she asked.

"You're beautiful," he said in response, taking another sip of coffee, watching as her eyes warmed and her cheeks flushed a soft pink. She looked down at the table and bit her lip.

"Thanks," she said, shifting.

He felt the caffeine coursing in his veins, and was ready to take on what he needed to.

"We need to talk," he said. Her eyes grew apprehensive, but she remained quiet. He liked that. She trusted him, and was prepared for him to take the lead.

"First, work," he said. "I think it's best we avoid talking about work during our personal time. Business time for business, pleasure for pleasure. Your company works with my school to get us in the clear in time for summer budgeting and preparations for next school year. From now until then, we keep our relationship under wraps. Got it?"

She nodded, wide-eyed. "Absolutely."

He caught her gaze and dropped his voice. "We can make this work," he said.

She felt it, the deeper meaning implied, and the hope he injected in his statement. She nodded. "I agree," she whispered.

He leaned forward. "We meet with your consulting company again next week," he said. "We'll spend time here at my place, or yours if you prefer, but we'll keep going out to a minimum, and when we do, we'll be discreet about it. There's no need for us to hide, but we should also use discretion. Agreed?"

She nodded again. He saw the tension go out of her as she sat back and sipped her coffee. He felt a pulse of pleasure. This is what he loved, the ability to take charge and bring peace to her. He would talk with her. But he would lead. And she was demonstrating the ability—desire, even—to follow.

"Good girl," he murmured on impulse. She smiled. He loved how eager she was to please, and the way she warmed under his praise. He would remember that.

"Doesn't mean we won't have issues come up," he said. "Let's be honest. This is a complicated situation. But we can work through this."

She smiled and nodded.

"Second," he said. "I'm going to ease you into ground rules." He watched as she squirmed a bit on her chair, and he suspected he knew what she was feeling—maybe a bit of apprehension as he stepped things up, but excitement, too. "Just the basics for now, honey. I don't want to overwhelm you."

She nodded. "Okay," she whispered.

He put his coffee down and reached for her chin. It was a dominant, intimate move, one that would get her undivided attention. He looked into her warm blue eyes, his fingers gently lifting her chin. She swallowed.

"It's important you talk to me throughout this, Heidi." She nodded, a slight pull of her chin in his hand. "I don't want you to feel overwhelmed or pressured. The idea of having rules is to help both me and you."

Her brows furrowed and he released her chin.

"Talk to me," he urged.

"I can see how it helps me," she said. "Knowing you're focusing on me, and..." her voice dropped and she grew shy. "Taking care of me," she said. "But how does it help *you?*"

God, she was cute.

He leaned back in his chair and crossed his arms over his chest. "Haven't you figured out by now I like bossing you around?" he teased. She rolled her eyes, but she was smiling. "No, really, hon," he said. "You having rules helps me because I know you're doing your best to take care of yourself when I'm not there. I like knowing you're safe, and making good choices, and doing what I've asked you." He paused, letting the import of his next sentence settle softly. "I like being obeyed." She nodded, and he could tell his answer pleased her.

He grew stern. "First." He paused. Her eyes widened as he continued. "No disobedience. If I tell you to do something, you will obey me. You're allowed to respectfully discuss things, of course, but I expect obedience." She nodded. He wondered what effect the word *obey* had on her. Some submissives would find it grated on them, but others would be attracted to obedience. Time would tell.

"Can you give me an example?" she asked, curiosity and apprehension in her eyes as she twisted a strand of hair between her fingers. "Like, what kinds of things will you tell me to do?"

"Sure," he said. "Maybe I think you've spent too much time on your phone and you need rest, so I may tell you it's time for bed, or that you need to get more sleep. I might ask you to wear a specific outfit. When I call your name, I want you to put down what you're doing and come to me. I'll expect you defer to me with major decisions, but we'll talk all this through."

"This carries over in bed?" she blurted out, looking surprised at herself. He chuckled.

"Of course," he responded with a slow smile. "*Especially* in bed." Her eyes warmed and she shifted on her chair.

"But not just bed?"

He crossed his arms across his chest. "Absolutely not." She inhaled.

"So you expect me to do whatever you say, whenever you say it."

He nodded. "More or less, but you always talk to me. If you have a problem or question, you tell me. It's important we communicate as effectively as possible. And that takes us to what's next."

"Okay," she said. He reached for her hand and gave it a quick squeeze.

"It's best if you get into the habit of saying 'Yes, sir' when we're alone, and you're expected to show me obedience, baby," he said, as gently as possible. She squirmed, but her eyes flamed.

"Yes, sir," she whispered. He felt himself grow hard. Shit, he could feel the tension rising, his need to have her again. He glanced quickly at the clock. Not enough time. Dammit.

They needed it to be Friday already.

He nodded. "Next. I expect you to treat me respectfully. No raising your voice, talking back, or sassing me." His voice dropped. "Understood?"

"Yes, sir," she said. He felt pleased at her acquiescence.

"This one goes both ways, honey," he said. "I expect you to treat me respectfully, but will respect you as well."

"Thank you," she whispered. He smiled.

"And last," he said. "Your safety. You're not to do anything I deem dangerous. No speeding, or screwing around with your phone in the car, or anything that could potentially hurt you. I'll explain my expectations when you go out at night, and safety things I expect you to be careful with at home. Am I clear on this?" he said, his voice taking on a hard edge. This was one he planned on implementing shortly, as it had become clear she had some habits that needed changing.

"I… well…" she sighed. "I can't use my phone in the car?" she asked, her eyebrows lifted. She frowned. Was she kidding?

"No!" he stated emphatically. "Not only is it dangerous, texting while driving is against state law," he said, surprised at the fact this wasn't obvious to her.

Her eyes flashed at him. "But my phone is my lifeline, Dom! And *everyone* uses their cell phones in the car. That's ridiculous!"

She pulled her hands back and crossed them, anger flashing in her eyes.

"It's not ridiculous," he stated, his voice deepening, and he knew she could hear the edge it took on, "and I'm warning you now, your tone needs to change. You sit your ass in your car, this is your new routine. Lock all the doors. Buckle your belt. Your phone gets zipped in your bag. Period. And if I find out you forgot any of those, I'll spank your ass."

"*What?*" she hissed. He hadn't expected she'd resist him so strongly on this, but his instincts kicked in. Safety rules were non-negotiable, and she *would* obey him.

"Come here," he instructed, pushing his seat back hard so that the chair legs scraped on the floor and he had ample room. She blinked. "*Now.*"

She came slowly to her feet, shuffling forward until she stood in front of him.

He grasped her waist and pulled her over his lap, pinning her into place with one firm hand on her lower back as his other raised.

"Do I have your attention now?" he asked.

"Yesss," she moaned.

"Good. I'm not exactly sure you know how serious I am about this," he began. "Or how much your safety means to me." He'd hoped she would get his point, but the way she kicked her feet showed she hadn't.

"These new rules are over the top!" she shouted. "Too much!" She gasped as he wasted no time in landing a hard, stinging swat to her bottom.

"You will speak to me respectfully," he instructed. "No yelling at me." He raised his hand and brought it down hard, a sound spank that reverberated around the kitchen. She yelped. He raised his hand again. "I don't care if you think you can multi-task with the best of them. You will take your safety seriously, even if I need to warm your ass every single time you take a seat in your car." *Whack!* "Do you understand me?"

"Yes—yes, sir! I get it! *Fine!*"

Another hard swat.

"Ow!"

He gave her three more stinging swats in rapid succession before he raised her to her feet in front of him. Her face was reddened, and her hands immediately went to her bottom, rubbing and looking not unlike a petulant child.

"Do we have an understanding, little girl?" he growled. She blinked, and he could tell by the look in her eyes she was chastened. Embarrassed, but chastened. This was one area he would not compromise.

"Yes, sir," she said, meekly.

"Good," he said, pulling her close to him so that she stood between his legs. The damn *time*. He looked at the clock on the wall. He let a beat pass before he spoke, allowing her to absorb what had just happened. "You okay?" he asked.

She nodded. "That's so confusing," she murmured.

"What's that?" he asked, his own hands reaching for her warmed backside, and rubbing.

"That's… embarrassing? Gosh, it's mortifying," she said. "But it's also really…" she paused and she sighed. "God, you're hot."

Dom arrived home significantly earlier than he usually did. With work wrapped up in the office, he was eager to set things up for the evening he planned with Heidi.

The idea had come to him over a text conversation she'd begun earlier in the day.

So… what kinds of things do you like, anyway? I mean… I know you like spanking. But are you into… other things?

It was his lunch break when the text came in. He'd methodically chewed through an entire bag of pretzels, a large Italian sub, an apple, and yogurt cup before replying to her.

Things… what exactly are we talking about here?

Um, I don't know… the things they talk about in books.

Like chains and handcuffs? Hot wax? Violet wands? Suspension systems? Sensory deprivation hoods? Gags? Be specific, baby.

O.M.G. I don't know what half those things are, and the other half scares the hell out of me.

He chuckled to himself.

There are many different… flavors, of dominance and submission, Heidi. You have Domestic Discipline, and standard D/s relationships. You have baby girls and Daddy Doms, and Masters and Slaves, then you've got the entire BDSM scene at your disposal.

Just… wow. Yikes.

There's… something for everyone.

Well, how do I know what I like?

He smiled to himself.

I can show you.

He felt like Aladdin on his magic carpet; hand stretched magnanimously out to the vast array below.

Okay. I mean, Yes, sir. I'd like to see.

Well that worked out just fine, because he wanted to show her.

When he arrived home, he knew she had another half hour at the office before she'd be heading home. He sent her another quick text.

I want you to text me before you leave the office. After you send the text, put your phone in your bag and close it tightly. Put your bag behind your seat. Don't forget to buckle, and lock your doors. Obey the speed limit, and come straight to me after you walk Princess. I want you dressed in a skirt, no panties.

Um. Yikes. Yes, sir.

He frowned at her response.

Overwhelmed? Irritated? Or just processing it all? Time

would tell. He changed into casual clothes, but spent some time standing in front of his closet. He removed several long, silk ties he rarely wore, and draped them across his bed. Before he turned from the closet, he reached for one of the hooks to the far right, where a thin, worn belt hung. He took it off the hook and draped it on the bed. That would do well, along with the other small items he'd picked up on his way home.

He saw her car pull into the parking lot, and a short while later, watched her return with Princess and bring her back to her apartment. Anticipation built. He would watch her, observe her reactions to what he asked and what he did. Playing in the BDSM scene was one thing, as was playing with bedroom dominance. What would it be like to be her full-time dominant?

His pulse quickened when he heard her tentative knock, at the same time he got a text from Matteo.

Dude. Dinner at Tony's. Tonight? Dom groaned. Shoving his phone in his pocket, he opened the door. She smiled shyly as he opened it and gestured for her to come in. He took her hand and led her to the living room just as his phone buzzed a second time. Silencing it, he tossed it on the table by the couch. He turned, walking to the couch where she stood waiting for him, sat down heavily, and pulled her onto his lap. He sighed as she nestled against his chest, and he pulled her close.

"Feels like it's been a while since I've seen you," he said, low. She murmured in assent. He reached his hand to the clip that held her hair in and pinched it, releasing the fragrant mass of chocolate brown waves. He tossed the clip to the side and pulled her head down. "Did you do what I asked? You followed your driving rules, and wore what I told you?"

"Yes, sir," she said, nestling in.

"How did you feel about all of that, baby?" he asked, as he held her. He could see her soften at the word *baby*. He suspected he had a bit of a baby girl on his lap. She liked his dominance.

She liked being taken care of. He would play that up and see how she responded.

"Well, the phone thing bugged me, to be honest," she said. "But I did what you said, and it felt different. I locked the doors and buckled, texted you and put my phone away. Then I felt like I was really focused on driving, and not trying to do more than one thing at a time. It felt weird, but not in a bad way."

"Very good," he said. "And the clothes?"

"Um, not wearing panties feels really naughty."

"Have you been naughty today?" he asked with a raised eyebrow, knowing the question would make her squirm, but turn her on.

"Not yet," she answered, nestling in closer. He chuckled.

His phone, silenced, lit up again on the side table.

"Do you need to get that?" she asked. He gave a curt nod.

"I want you to kneel here," he said. "On the floor in front of me, kneel and put your hands in my lap while I get these messages. I've gotta make it clear I'm busy tonight."

She slid obediently off his lap, a strange look crossing her face as she knelt. Her eyes went from side to side and she looked guarded in a way she hadn't a moment before. But when her knees hit the floor and her hands went to his lap, the look faded and she looked calmer. He picked up his phone.

Plans tonight. Can't make it.

He put it down, and reached a finger under her chin.

"You like it when I call you baby," he asked, more of a statement than a question. She swallowed and nodded. "Stand and go get the brown bag I have on my desk. Bring it here."

She stood and obeyed, getting the bag and bringing it back quickly.

"Good, baby, now kneel again," he instructed.

She obeyed. He removed the flat wooden hairbrush he'd purchased and put the bag on the couch next to him. Her eyes widened, but she said nothing.

"Don't be nervous, honey," he said. He dropped his voice. "Unless you did something I need to punish you for?"

"No! No, sir," she said, shaking her head. He smiled.

"Well, let's test it out just in case I *do* need to use it," he said. Her eyes widened.

"Test it out?" she squeaked. He'd only ever punished her with his hand, but she was ready to try something new, and he was curious where her tolerance was. He'd spanked her very firmly with his hand, and knew that if he needed to discipline her, his hand would likely do just fine. But she might like the thuddy feel of the brush, or the stingy feel of the belt he had for her in his bedroom.

"Go over to my desk," he instructed, "and bend over."

He heard the catch of breath as she stood and stepped over to his desk. She placed her hands gingerly on top, bent over and stuck her bottom out. He smiled. So sweet. He placed the brush on the desk next to her, and she jumped.

"Relax," he said. "You're not in trouble. Just trust me. Try to focus on what you feel, and just do what I say."

She nodded.

"I'm going to spank you, Heidi," he said gently. "I'm going to warm you up first. If I spank you with my hand, you'll be primed to take more."

"Yeah, okay," she said. He brought his hand down in a sharp swat that had a punitive edge.

"What was that?"

"Yes, sir!"

"Good," he said, giving her another swat. She wore a loose-fitting denim skirt that hugged her curves but had ample room to move. He lifted it and smiled to himself. She had obeyed him. He gave her a few more swats with his hand, until she was lightly red and warm to the touch. She inhaled and tensed when he picked up the brush.

"Tonight, you'll focus on obeying my instructions," he said, as he lifted the brush and brought it down firmly, but not harshly. He'd tested it on his hand and it though it was wide and flat, the wood was light and unfinished, making it effective for spanking, but something that would be good to begin with. He'd used heavier, varnished paddles at The Club, and knew the heft and sting of them would deliver a much harder spanking than Heidi was ready for.

She hissed as the wood connected, but she maintained her position. "You'll tell me if anything scares you, but you'll also tell me when you like something. Understood?" *Swat!*

"Yes, sir."

He gave her half a dozen firmer swats. She took them all, in perfect position. He pulled her skirt down, and she looked over her shoulder at him. She looked disappointed.

"Are you done?" she asked.

"For now," he said. He took her by the hand and brought her back over to the couch, pulling her onto his lap, brush still in hand. "This is a good tool to have," he said, as he drew it through her long hair, and she sighed in contentment. "I can use it to help you relax, while I brush your hair. But if you're a naughty little girl, I can use it to spank your ass." She shifted. Yes, she liked the naughty girl image.

"Are you a naughty girl, Heidi?" he whispered in her ear. She licked her lips, and he felt himself grow hard with her bottom nestled up against him.

"I can be," she whispered. "I think I need someone to make me behave." Her eyes closed as he continued to brush her hair, and he felt her grow heavier as she leaned back against him. "Are you up for the challenge?" she asked drunkenly.

"Hell yeah," he said, and as he continued to brush her hair, he heard her stomach growl.

"You hungry, baby?" he asked.

"Starving," she groaned.

"When was the last time you ate?" He brought the brush through her hair again, and her hair gleamed in the light.

"Um…" her voice trailed off. He felt a twinge of irritation.

"You don't remember?"

"Well, I ate breakfast with you…" she said, her eyes opening, and looking at him sideways. "But I worked through lunch. I think Paul ordered out, but he got burgers and fries and I'm trying to watch my weight." He put the brush down and spun her around.

"Not cool," he said, taking her chin firmly and making her look at him. "You can't skip meals. I want you eating normal meals, and no skipping."

"Oh." She nodded, chastened. "Yes, sir."

He reached out and smoothed the hair off her forehead. "I think you've got a baby girl in there, honey," he said gently. "You like when I take care of you. You like sitting on my lap and having your hair brushed."

She bit her lip. "Okay. I'm not sure what that means, but I believe you."

He nodded. "The thought of me punishing you for being a naughty girl," he said. "How does that feel to you? Does it irritate you? Or do you like the idea of me protecting you? Let's say, for example, you got a spanking for not going to bed when I told you. What do you think of that?" She kept her eyes focused on him.

"Hot," she whispered. He nodded.

"That's what I thought," he whispered back, tucking a stray lock behind her ear. "You like being my baby girl," he said. "We're going to get something to eat, and we'll try a few more things while we're out. Sound good, baby?"

She grinned. "Sounds great."

Looked like they'd be going to Tony's after all.

Chapter 13

Heidi added her signature to one final document in the proposal she'd prepared, then closed the folder and slid her chair back with a satisfied sigh. Her eyes automatically sought out the clock above the door to the lobby. Four o'clock, which meant she had another hour before she'd promised Dom she'd leave. Four o'clock, which also meant she'd been working without interruption for two hours. Not too shabby.

Not so long ago, two hours of work wouldn't have even registered. Even a month ago, work was the thing she did from the time she opened her eyes (to begin compulsively checking her phone), until whatever time exhaustion forced her to push her laptop aside and roll over to sleep. But these days? Two hours was a record.

For one thing, her man (*Her man! A concept that never failed to make her belly flip!*) liked to text her at various times throughout the day—sometimes a quick hello to let her know she was on his mind, other times with strict reminders or sexy instructions he'd dreamed up just to torment her, just to make sure *he* was on *her* mind.

Like she could think about anything else.

Her concentration was shot. She'd be sitting in front of her computer, like she was now, ready to churn out a report… and the next thing she knew, she'd be staring at her own blank, goofy expression reflected in the black screen of a monitor that had *shut itself off* while she'd been daydreaming.

Thank God for Paul, she thought, as she clicked to open their project management app and noted that all of their active projects were on-track. He'd been pulling more than his fair share of weight around here recently.

When he isn't busy acting as my therapist and D/s guru, of course, she thought wryly. Those early days had been full of freakouts and gushing wide-eyed wonder.

Paul, he says he suspects I'm a 'baby girl' so I just Googled, and… ohmygod!

Dom texted again! Says he wants me to drive carefully on my way home so that 'my baby comes back to me safely'. I can't even explain how amazing it feels to know I'm that important to someone!

Seriously, Paul, do not *compliment me on this blouse—it barely fits across my chest and I keep having to yank it up. But how can I tell him that I don't like him picking my clothes? He's going to be so mad.*

Hey, if you're ordering from Roadhouse, can you get me a burger? I know! I never get that stuff, but… Dom says my curves are exactly where he likes them and I'm not allowed to starve myself. I just love the way that man takes care of me.

I can't call him 'Sir.' You have no idea how hard it is, especially when I'm mad. But when I tell him, he just smiles and reminds me that I'm his good girl and that I need to focus. What is that even about? *I just don't know if I'm cut out for this.*

She couldn't imagine talking to anyone else about this stuff. Certainly not anyone currently in her life. Her sister would no doubt be horrified. Her father would murder Dom. Her mother… well, her mother would have Heidi committed for agreeing to this in the first place!

But Paul had stoically endured her sentimental gabbing and had handled every freakout with patience, restraint, and the never-ending mantra, *"Have you talked to Dom about this, Heids?"*

That last bit had been kind of infuriating.

"Paul, you're supposed to be *my* friend, on *my* side," she'd finally told him, outraged that he refused to see how high-handed Dom was being about one thing or another. "Is there some kind of *dom code?* You're not allowed to criticize one another or you lose your membership?"

But Paul had simply sipped his coffee calmly and thoughtfully, and broken the whole thing down for her in a few simple words.

"Heidi, if we receive a contract with conditions you don't like, you sometimes ask my feedback or my advice, but you don't come and bitch to me about it. You've never once done that. Why?"

Heidi had blown out a breath and admitted, "Because *you* can't do anything to change it. Yeah, yeah, I get it."

But Paul had shaken his head.

"Not just that, Heids. It's because bitching is what people do when they feel *powerless*, and when it comes to this stuff," a quick gesture that encompassed all the papers and folders on her desk, "you know you're *not*. If you really want a contract, if you know it's what's best for the company, you'll adjust your projections to make the client's terms work for you. If you really can't handle the terms, you'll tell them so, and nine times out of ten, *they* will adjust their terms because they want you to work on their project and they want you to be happy. *Being a submissive doesn't mean you're powerless.* Just think about it."

And just like that, the whole situation had snapped into focus.

Just because she was naturally inclined to be submissive didn't mean submitting was always supposed to be easy! And it was not a one-time decision—it was something she would have to choose every single day. Multiple times a day. If she wanted to please

Dom, and *God did she want that*, then she would choose to step out of her comfort zone, and choose to *trust him*.

And that meant doing something that was, for her, even harder than trying to follow his every dictate without question. It meant opening up to him, sharing which aspects of their relationship she enjoyed and which she struggled with, so that they had a relationship that worked for both of them.

"You like letting me lead you, honey," he'd told her. "And in the same way, I like taking care of you. How can I do that if you don't tell me what's going on in that head of yours? You're not a robot. I don't expect this shit to be easy for you, and maybe you need a chance to ease into things. That's fine. What this relationship looks like today isn't what it's going to look like five years from now. Just keep talking to me, keep trusting me, keep working at it. When I know you struggle, but I see you choose to submit? That's beautiful, baby."

And it *was* beautiful.

But the idea that they'd be together five years from now, still working things out? That was beauty beyond anything she'd imagined.

She had never known that happiness like this existed. She'd always imagined that romance novels set an impossible standard, an unattainable fantasy. Now, she knew that the words on the page could never do justice to the reality. It was fun, it was hot, but it also nourished something inside her that she hadn't known was starving.

They'd gone out to dinner with his brothers several times, and both guys, especially Tony, had been quick to welcome her to the family—joking, talking, and teasing her like the big brothers she might have had in some parallel-universe family that was more apt to rough-house and clown around than to plan political protests. They'd even asked her—*commanded her*, more like, since Dom's brothers had both inherited that same way of stating a request as a royal decree—to invite Hillary down over the holiday weekend for a barbecue.

True to his word, Dom hadn't asked a single question about the Easterbrook analysis or the recommendations she'd make to the board. She knew it weighed on him, knowing that his staff or his students might take a hit, but he was determined not to let that shadow their relationship, and, as he'd told her gruffly, he knew she was damn good at her job and trusted her to do it right. Still, not long after their initial meeting, Heidi had officially handed the entire file off to Paul to handle at his own discretion. It was simply too hard to be impartial, and this relationship was too new and too important to her to risk—*more* important, in the long run, than personally overseeing the audit.

When she'd told Dom, he hadn't made a comment... he'd simply brought out a new toy—a small, black leather flogger, and after giving her the most intense, sensual spanking she'd had yet, proceeded to make her climax harder than she ever had in her life.

She squirmed in her seat just thinking about it.

Unlike the incident at the school last week, which had made her squirm for an entirely different reason.

She and Dom had been on their way home from the gym last Saturday when he realized that he'd left his spare phone charger in his desk at work and decided to swing by to get it. As he'd led her by the hand down the dark, empty corridor to his office, all dark and serious and *Dom*, she'd been seized by the need to see him smile, make him lose that business-like composure.

"Principal Angelico?" she'd simpered in her best little-girl voice, pulling her hand away from his to lean dramatically against the bank of lockers that lined the hall outside his office. "I'm awfully nervous about this! I didn't *mean* to break the rules!"

She'd bitten her lip and batted her eyelashes beseechingly, while running a hand across the thin tank top that covered her breasts.

He'd frozen solid, one eyebrow raised, and she'd thought for a moment that he wouldn't play along. But then his lips had pursed like he was fighting a smile, and she knew she'd won.

"Miss Morrow," he'd said, stroking his chin appraisingly as his eyes lit up. "You broke the rules, didn't you?"

"Well, yes, sir, I suppose I did… it's just…" A pause while she ran her fingertips up and down her stomach, his eyes watching her every move. "I try *so hard* to be a *good girl*, sir."

He'd smirked at that, even as he stalked closer, leaning in to tower over her.

"I'm sure you do, Miss Morrow. But you've been very, *very* naughty… And I can't have naughty girls going unpunished, can I?" The last words breathed in her ear, tightened her nipples.

"No, sir," she'd told him truthfully, as his teeth clenched down on her earlobe.

And just as she'd been about to tell him what she'd do to make amends for her naughtiness…

The freakin' office door had opened, and they'd barely had time to jump apart before Jay Fucking Divris had walked out!

It had taken some fast talking on Dom's part to explain their presence at the school—Heidi had lost a thumb drive the other day, thought it might have gotten mixed up in Dom's papers, so he'd agreed to let her have a quick look around…

On a Saturday.

Dressed in gym clothes.

With one car in the parking lot.

She wasn't sure that Jay bought it, but he hadn't said a word. And after he'd left, Dom had taken the opportunity to show her, *with the phone charger cord*, what happened to naughty girls who tried to seduce their doms at their places of business.

Ouch.

She couldn't plug her phone in at night without remembering, and judging from the leering grin Dom gave her each night as she slid into his bed, he hadn't forgotten either.

A knock on the frame of the open door nearly had her jumping out of her seat, her reverie forgotten.

"Hey, Heids, got a minute?"

Paul came in without waiting for a reply, brow furrowed and flawless brown hair standing on end.

"Yeah, definitely," Heidi assured him. "Just doing that staring-into-space thing… *again*."

He'd caught her at it more than once and had teased her relentlessly, but today he didn't crack a smile as he took his seat.

"What's up?" she asked, concerned now. "Everything okay with your family? With John?"

She'd been happy to see that Paul's love life had taken an upswing just as things with her and Dom had settled down, and she hoped his fledgling relationship wasn't responsible for the frown on his face.

Paul looked startled.

"Oh, yeah. John is fine, we're… fine." He waved a hand dismissively. "It's actually…"

He blew out a breath and hesitated… behavior so unlike his usual calm, no-bullshit attitude that Heidi felt a knot form in the pit of her stomach.

"Tell me!" she instructed.

Paul nodded and reluctantly placed a folder on top of her desk.

"Easterbrook?" she asked, glancing at the label. "You've been reconciling the budgets with the accounts to see if there is any surplus that could offset the loss of income from the alumni, right? I read your updated notes in the project tracker. What did you find?"

It was hard not to get excited at the prospect of a surplus. She knew the problem wouldn't be that easy to solve—they might find a couple of thousand in surplus, not nearly enough to make up the hundreds of thousands of shortfall. Still, every penny helped. Frankly, she'd joked with Paul that she'd consider throwing the mother of all bake sales, or raffling off a car, if that would get them one step closer to closing the gap without cutting salaries or scholarships.

But Paul didn't answer her question right away.

"Jay sent me the updated financials for this month," he began, shifting in his seat, his eyes on the folder.

"Right. Okay… and? Has something changed from what was projected?" she asked, when he didn't continue.

"Actually… yes," he admitted. "The alumni donation numbers were up. Way above what we had noted in our projections."

Heidi felt her eyes widen.

"But that's great news! By how much? Enough to matter? Can I cancel the bake sale?" she joked.

But once again, Paul didn't return her smile, and he still wouldn't meet her eyes.

"What, Paul? Will you please spit it out? I suck at playing guessing games," she begged.

Her phone buzzed on the desk between them, and both of them looked at the display.

How's my girl?

With a look at Paul, who somehow seemed to grow even tenser, she grabbed the phone and typed a quick reply.

Doing very well. Half hour until departure.

Perfect. Don't be late, baby. I have plans.

Despite Paul's weirdness, Heidi couldn't help smiling as she set the phone back down.

"How much do you know about this guy, Heidi?" Paul asked suddenly, sounding like a disapproving older brother.

"Who? Dom?" The question, especially coming from Paul, was so startling she wasn't sure how to reply. "Since when are you concerned about Dom?"

"Since right now. I mean, you overheard this guy having sex with this never-ending *cavalcade* of women—"

"Cavalcade?" she scoffed. "He didn't do monogamy before me. I didn't do D/s *at all*, so what?"

"And then suddenly he steps right in and starts domming you left and right, all up in your business…"

"All up in my… Are you kidding me? You're the one who told me—"

"And then, next thing you know, *oops,*" he threw his hands in the air dramatically, his eyes wild. "We're investigating *his* school, and *haha!* we didn't even trade last names before we *jumped into bed* and no one knew that there would be this whole *conflict of interest!*"

His words hit her like a blow to the solar plexus, but she rebounded.

"Conflict of interest? How? There's *no* conflict of interest, because I passed the files to *you!*"

"But it doesn't look that way from the outside!" he exploded, standing up and dragging a hand through his hair. "It's not enough to avoid impropriety, we have to avoid even the *appearance* of impropriety if we want to maintain our reputation! And as soon as someone finds out about you and Dom the dominant, everything we've built evaporates!"

Paul paced in front of the desk like a caged animal. Paul, who considered it a massive overreaction to even raise his voice, who had literally *never* lost his temper in all the years they'd worked together, no matter how ridiculous or demanding a client was, who kept his cool no matter how freaked out Heidi herself became, had completely lost it. And seeing him like this somehow helped her rein her own temper in and tie the pieces together.

"You found something bad," she said calmly, as the facts finally slid into place in her mind. "Okay. So what *exactly* did you find?"

He exhaled and sat down, all the energy draining from him at once, and he pulled two sheets of paper from the folder.

"This," he set the first piece of paper down in front of her, "is the quarterly statement they initially provided us."

"I recognize it," Heidi agreed, scanning the sheet.

"And this," he placed the second paper to the right of the first, "is the monthly sheet we just received. From *Dom's office.*"

Heidi compared the two pages and tried to ignore the emphasis Paul had placed on the last two words.

"It looks like... the carryover balance is too high? The opening numbers on the monthly report should match the ending numbers from the quarterly report, and they don't."

She glanced up at Paul, who nodded.

"So... someone made an error," she concluded with a shrug, gathering the sheets together. "Honestly, Paul. We'll just ask them to check the numbers and..."

"I've done that," Paul said flatly, folding his arms across his chest. "Louisa sent me copies, I followed up with her a second time. The numbers on this monthly report are the same numbers in the official quarterly report file on the school's server... the only discrepancy is in *our* copy of the quarterly reports."

"Okaaay..." Heidi rubbed her temple, the beginnings of a headache forming. "How could that happen?"

"It shouldn't happen at all. The finance department prepares the quarterly numbers and presents them to the headmaster for approval. Once the file is marked approved, it can't be changed... at least in theory. Hard copies are sent to the headmaster, the finance department, and the head of the Board of Directors... and, in this case, to us," he added. "But the electronic record is stored on the school's server. Authorized people can access it, print it, copy it... but they can't change it. It's encrypted and password protected."

Heidi nodded. "Right, that makes sense. Then how was it changed?"

"One administrator has access, Heids," Paul said gently. And the answer settled like an anvil in her stomach.

Dom. As headmaster, of course Dom would be the one with access to the file.

"You're saying that—possibly for a very good and logical reason that we haven't discovered yet—Dom may have updated the file?"

"I also confirmed with the finance department that the money indicated on the monthly report is an accurate reflection of the amount currently in the bank account. The finance department couldn't… or *wouldn't*… tell me more without authorization from the board, but money was transferred into the alumni donation account a week ago, and the file was updated at the same time."

"Someone *deposited* money?" Heidi asked.

Paul nodded.

'Looks like someone was trying to put some money in there, and then cover their tracks by going back and updating the quarterlies. And it was a pretty thorough cover-up, too. The hard copies of the quarterlies that should be on file in the finance department, the headmaster's office, and with the board have all gone missing. We may have the only remaining copies of the original quarterly reports."

"But… why? Why would someone do that?"

He shrugged. "They could have been trying to buy some time, or maybe hoping the board would stop us from poking around if they could make up part of the budget shortfall? I don't know. But, Heidi… The person I spoke to in finance let it slip that the name on the transfer request was Dominic Angelico."

She closed her eyes briefly and then spoke as clearly and confidently as she could.

"They're wrong. Or you're missing something."

"The Internal Review Board for Admissions," he continued mercilessly, "has exactly three members—the teacher with the most seniority, a seventy-year-old English Lit teacher who doesn't understand how to work email; the head of the finance department, Jay Divris, who happens to be the son of the board's most senior member; and the headmaster of the school. It had to be one of those people involved in the bribery scam in the first place. And honey, my money is not on the English teacher."

"What you're suggesting... it's not possible, Paul."

"No, honey," he said in that same gentle voice, dropping his hands to the desk and leaning forward in his chair. "It's the *only* possibility. And I'm so sorry—I can't tell you how sorry I am—but you've got to see that it's the truth."

Objectively speaking, he made a damn good point—what were the chances that all these signs would point to an innocent man? What were the chances that she'd start dating her neighbor the same week she started investigating his school? But every cell of her body—every single one, even the cells that wondered if this was all too good to be true, and the ones that worried that she was too curvy or too demanding or not submissive enough to please Dom—rejected what Paul had said. That simply wasn't Dom. It wasn't in him to be... sneaky.

"Paul, a month ago I would have believed you. Heck, I would have come to that conclusion even before you did. But you know, *you know*, that you can't be with someone the way I've been with Dom and not know that it's... real."

Paul huffed impatiently, a teacher with a recalcitrant student who refused to see the answer.

"Then tell me how it happened, Heidi. Because, I swear, I have looked at this every way I know how, and I can't see how anyone else could have done it."

Heidi leaned forward and placed her hands on the desk.

"Couldn't someone else have the password?" she asked.

Paul shook his head.

"Dom's not stupid," he argued. "I'm guessing he doesn't go around giving out his password. And before you suggest it," he held up a hand to stop her from interrupting, "I'm also sure he's smart enough to have changed his password from 1-2-3-4."

Heidi *had* been about to say that. Drat.

"Okay, well, maybe he told someone he trusted? Maybe he told Louisa... or Jay!" she suggested. And once she had said his name, then a possible scenario formed in her mind.

Paul shook his head again and started to stand, but Heidi grabbed his hand and stopped him.

"*Wait*, Paul, wait!" she cried. "*Listen.* Jay was in Dom's office the other day! Dom and I showed up at the school—uh, unexpectedly—on a Saturday... and he was coming out of the headmaster's office! I mean, for all I know, he does that every Saturday, but... what if he used Dom's computer and Dom... I dunno... had the password saved on there?"

Paul sighed.

"You're clutching at straws, Heids."

"Paul, why don't we just *ask* Dom?"

Paul frowned, then shook his head.

"I don't think it would look very good for us to tip off someone who may be involved before the board has a chance to investigate. I want to believe he's innocent, Heidi, for your sake and because I genuinely like the guy. But things are kind of stacked against him. It's out of our hands now."

"You're going to turn this over to the board and you're asking me to keep it from him? His job is at stake, his professional reputation. I can't do that, Paul," she argued.

"I'm asking you to do just what you intended when you handed me the files, honey," he said, and his tone was gentle but brooked no argument. "To eliminate any conflict of interest, trust me to handle the audit and prepare the information for the board."

She shook her head stubbornly.

"I need to know you're going to keep looking into this, Paul. I need to know you're not going to turn over this incriminating stuff without digging just a little bit deeper."

Paul looked at her with narrowed eyes for a moment.

"This is the real deal for you," he said. "Isn't it? With Dom."

Heidi bit her lip and nodded. "Yeah," she said.

After a moment, Paul nodded too.

"All right. Fine. I guess maybe this *is* just a little *too* neatly packaged. I'll give Dom the benefit of the doubt and keep digging. But in the meantime, don't do anything…"

Heidi's phone rang shrilly, interrupting the conversation, and her eyes flew automatically to the clock. Five-fifteen. *Shit*. She grabbed the phone and accepted the call.

"Hi, honey," she said automatically, her eyes still pleading with Paul. "I'm running—"

"Heidi? Heidi, it's me, Mom."

"Mom?"

God, of all the times to forget to check the display before accepting the call.

"Listen, Mom, it's not a good time right now, can I—"

"Heidi, it's your sister! I don't know what to do! She's been kidnapped by some-some… *predator* who wants to keep her as his *sex slave*!"

Her mother was screaming loud enough for Paul to hear, judging by the way he straightened, instantly on alert.

"Mom, calm down," Heidi said, as Paul leaned over the desk to better hear the conversation. "What happened to Hillary?"

"She's disappeared! *Kidnapped*!"

Only years of experience with her mother's overreactions made it possible for Heidi to stay calm. More than likely, Hillary had spent the night with a boyfriend and forgotten to tell their mother… more likely still, Hillary *had* told her, and their mother had forgotten as she jetted off to save the emus, or some-such.

"What makes you think she's been kidnapped, Mom? Have you called the police?"

"Oh, the *police*," her mother scoffed. "Useless! Just like when I tried to tell them about that factory with the toxic waste and they—"

"Mom, you've got to focus," Heidi instructed. "What did the police say about *Hillary*?"

"They said she's over eighteen, and it seems like it was consensual, and they're not going to do a damn thing. But I know my daughters, Heidi, and I know it could not *possibly* have been consensual!"

Paul looked at her with wide eyes and shook his head. *Is this for real?*

Heidi looked at him helplessly and grimaced. *I have no idea!* She took a deep breath, trying to rein in her patience.

"*What* was consensual, Mom?" Heidi demanded.

"I called Hillary yesterday, and her roommate, Daphne, said that she was out on a *date*. And Hillary hadn't mentioned any men to me!"

Because she's smarter than that, Heidi thought. *Nothing like getting grilled about your guy's stance on feminism and global warming before you've had your first date.*

"So, I told Daphne to have her call me when she came home, and she didn't call, not last night *or* this morning!"

"She has classes, Mom. She's a senior in college, and she—"

"I'm *aware* of that, Heidi," her mother said impatiently. "But this morning *Daphne* called *me* because Hillary hadn't come home last night, and she wasn't answering her cell phone. And *Daphne* was worried!"

Heidi exchanged an anxious glance with Paul. If Daphne was worried, the situation had just become more serious.

"Daphne said that Hillary met a man *on the Internet*," her mother continued. "He was a *total stranger*. And his name is *Marauder*. Who calls themselves Marauder, Heidi? *Who*?"

Paul's eyes widened. *Marauder?*

"Oh, God. Doesn't she know how many rapes and murders there are every day?" her mother moaned.

"I'm sure she does, Mom. She's a smart girl," Heidi said, even as she felt herself starting to panic. *Didn't* Hillary know how stupid that was? *God.*

"Daphne said Hillary left her computer on, so she checked the messages and..." her mother inhaled deeply, then sobbed. "According to her last email, she was planning to take the train to Boston to meet him at some club... *Black Box.* It's a *sex* club! And the things he said... Oh! He was going to *hurt* her, Heidi! And I just *know* Hillie would *never* agree to that!"

Paul sat up straight in his chair and motioned for Heidi to cover the phone.

"Hold on just one second, Mom," she said.

Paul wasted no time in relaying his bad news.

"Heidi, I've been to Black Box. *Once.* And that was enough. That is not a place for a newbies or even girls who like to be spanked once in a while, it's..." he hesitated, as if gauging how much to tell her. "It's serious kink. Deviant stuff. Was your sister into the scene?"

"Not that I know of!" Heidi exclaimed. "Hillie is all into hearts and romance and destiny and *forever love*! I can't even process this, Paul! What do I *do?*"

She tried to breathe normally, but the air kept catching in her throat. Despite her best efforts, she was gripped by panic. If the police couldn't do anything, how could they find Hillary?

Paul's eyes raked over her face. He narrowed his own eyes, then seemed to come to a decision. He grabbed his phone and began hitting buttons.

"Heidi? *Heidi!*" her mother screeched.

"I'm here, Mom," Heidi said. "Okay, you need to call Daphne and... have her forward all the messages to me. I'll-I'll see if anyone knows anything about this club or a guy called Marauder, okay? Can you do that, Mom?"

"I… yes, I can do that," her mother agreed, sniffling.

Before Heidi could hang-up, Paul motioned for her to hand him her phone.

She heard him soothing her mother with, "Hi, Frances? This is Paul," even as he passed his own phone to Heidi with a firm nod.

"Uh... Hello?" Heidi said.

"Baby?"

Dom. Oh, thank God.

"Heidi, honey, tell me what's going on. Paul said your sister is in trouble."

Heidi drew a shuddering breath.

"Dom, Hillie went off with someone, to some club. I have no idea whether she knew what she was getting herself into or not, but she's way too young to be going to sex clubs anyway, and what the hell was she thinking, meeting guys online? What the *hell* was she thinking, Dom? She's my baby sister and she's been missing since last night, and no one has seen her or knows a single thing about this guy who took her, and she won't answer her phone, and the *police won't help!* What do you do when the police won't *help you??*"

By the end, her voice was shrill enough to do her mother proud.

"All right, baby, here's what we're going to do. Are you listening?"

His deep voice was melodic and instantly soothing.

"I'm listening," she whispered.

"Paul is going to drive you home, okay? I'm going to make some calls, and I'm going to get this under control. Do you understand?"

"I… Dom, we need to *do* something. We can't just sit around making phone calls! My mom knows the name of the club Hillie went to—Black Box—I need to go over there, see if they've seen—"

"Heidi," his voice was firmer this time. Insistent. *Warning*. It was enough to break through the icy wall of terror that gripped her. "Under no circumstances are you to go *near* that place. Do you hear me? *I* will take care of this. You will not find your sister by putting yourself in danger. Do you understand?"

"Y-yes. Yes, I understand," Heidi said, hanging on to his voice like a lifeline.

"Come home to me, Heidi, and I will take care of everything," he vowed.

"O-okay," she agreed, with a nod he couldn't see.

"Tell me what I just said, my good girl," he said softly.

"Come home to you, and you'll take care of Hillie," she repeated.

"That's right, baby. I'll take care of Hillie, and I'll take care of you, too."

Chapter 14

Dom paced the small area in front of his desk, where he could look out the window and see the cars coming and going in the small parking lot outside his apartment. Maybe it had been a mistake, having Paul bring her to him. He should've gotten his ass in his own car and *gotten* her. But no, that made no sense. The club was closer to their apartments than her office, and he had phone calls to make. His phone buzzed. Paul was on his way.

Club *Fucking* Black Box. Her sister!

Dom and Matteo had ventured into the dark recesses of that club just once, on a cold night when Matteo had broken it off with a high-strung, completely plastered submissive who made returning to their usual club a momentary impossibility. Matteo hadn't wanted to go home, and had heard of Black Box from one of his cronies. Dom had gone reluctantly, curiosity pushing him past his initial reticence.

It was a dark place, secret and hidden, accessed only by invitation, which Matteo had secured via text shortly before their arrival. All members wore masks, per club regulations, and there was a heavier feel of secrecy than at the D/s hotspot Matteo and

Dom preferred, an institution so well-known and well-respected that it was known simply as The Club. The Club maintained privacy and discretion. Consent and legality prevailed. It was a completely different story at Black Box.

Dom was not at all surprised when Black Box had been given a hefty fine and temporary shut-down orders a few months prior when an undercover agent had revealed the club's insidious allowance of underage activity. But they brought in ample profit, had a top-notch legal team, and had reopened their doors after a mere slap-on-the-wrist.

His phone rang. Matteo. He breathed a sigh of relief, vowing to himself he'd never again tell Matteo he was a pain in the ass if he could pull through this one night.

"Dom. What the hell is going on?" There was none of his usual teasing. Dom's text had been straightforward and urgent.

"Don't know much yet," he continued, pacing quickly before he glanced out the window again. He needed to get the hell out and walk off his nervous energy. He grabbed the spare set of keys Heidi had given him, and decided he'd take Princess for her walk and give her dinner, so Heidi could have the evening free. As he made his way over to her apartment, he filled Matteo in. "Heidi's sister Hillary, younger sister, still in college. Wrapped up with some asshole from Black Box. She's gone in as of last night and no one's seen or heard from her since. Police won't get involved. She's of age and apparently consented."

Matteo swore. "You got a name on the guy?"

"Marauder. You familiar?"

"No, but it'll help when I make some calls."

Dom pushed the door to Heidi's apartment open, snapped his fingers as Princess reared back to greet him with a flying leap, and quickly snapped the leash on her. He patted her head obligingly, and took her back out to the front yard, his stern look commanding her to do her business and be quick about it. She got the message.

"Good," Dom said. "You've got an in there, right?"

"Yeah, there's a guy I went through basic training with who's a bouncer there now. Goes by Slay. He's not into that shit but stays on the outskirts. He owes me a favor. I'll reach out. If that doesn't work, I've got a few more people I can try to connect with."

After a quick walk around the lot, filling Matteo in with all he knew, he brought Princess back to the apartment, made sure her food and water was filled, and walked into Heidi's room.

"Much appreciated, man."

"Yeah, I've got this. I'm on my way over there now. You've got Heidi?"

Dom was just finishing putting her clean clothes in an overnight bag. He didn't want her running back to her place, not tonight.

He saw Paul's blue pickup swerve into the parking lot.

"She just got here."

"Keep your phone on. I'll want to ask her questions. What her sister looks like, shit like that."

"Got it."

"You owe me Roadhouse burgers for this."

Dom quirked a smile. "You get her sister outta there, I'll even let you get the onion rings this time."

Matteo chuckled in return.

Dom knew he thrived on this—the adrenaline pumping through his veins, the chance at a rescue. He also knew the joking didn't mean for a minute Matteo didn't take this seriously. Quite the opposite. He was fortifying himself for what very well could be a throw-down. He would get this shit done. It might not be pretty, but he'd do it.

Dom disconnected, shoved his phone in his back pocket, slung the bag over his shoulder, gave Princess a quick pat on the head, and ordered low, "You stay here and be a good girl and I'll get you some of those fake bacon things." Princess obediently lay on the floor as Dom left and locked the door behind him.

Paul pulled into a parking space and the passenger door flew open before he'd come to a complete halt. Dom clenched his jaw. Had she even been wearing a seat belt? Jesus. But he took a deep breath. Heidi needed calm right now, and it was not the time for him to get on her case about smaller matters. She took one look at him and ran.

"Oh my God, Dom," she said. He reached his arms for her as she crashed into him, her blue eyes panic-stricken. He hated seeing her like this. He felt his temperature rise. He wanted to beat the man who'd accosted her sister, the man responsible for the fear in his girl's eyes. God, he hoped Matteo would do a thorough job of it.

"I read the emails," she said, her voice dropping to a whisper. "He's a seducer. I can read right through it. He fed her every line! And what he planned to do to her. Oh my God! And Dom! It gets worse!" she said, her voice raising as she lifted her cell phone. "She sent me a text, while we were on the way over here, asking me to help her! I replied but then didn't hear back from her. He must have realized she had access to her phone and taken it."

He took the phone from Heidi's hands as Paul came around the car, hands stuck in his pockets. He watched Dom and Heidi with an odd look, as if he were pleased to see them together, but guarded.

"Let's go to my apartment," Dom said.

"Go to your apartment!" she fairly shouted. To his surprise, she pulled back, her hands pushing him off her so hard they slapped against his chest. "I'm not going to sit here while my sister is *kidnapped and tortured!* We need to go there, and we need to go there *now!*" Her eyes flashed, and she took a step backward, in the direction of Paul's truck. "There are two of you guys and one of me, and I'm so pissed off I could kill him myself. I swear to God! Let's go! Now!"

Dom knew in the moment that she was half-crazed with worry, and he knew he couldn't allow her emotions to rule her reason. Dom's eyes met Paul's, and Paul nodded. He clicked the lock on his keys, and his truck beeped. Heidi's eyes flew to Paul, furious. She fruitlessly tried to open the door. "Unlock your goddamn truck!"

Dom marched over to Heidi and took her hand. "Come with me," he ordered firmly.

"Dom!" she said, trying to pull her hand away from him, turning back to the truck. "*No*! I'm not going with you! We need to go *get* her!"

He quickly overpowered her in one move, letting go of her hand and grasping her wrist. He knew she was beyond reason. He also knew what she needed from him now was clear direction. Still, she pulled and twisted, refusing to go. Dom looked at Paul, took the bag off his shoulder, and Paul braced for the catch. Dom swung the bag over to Paul, and Paul caught it. Before she could realize what he was doing, Dom swept Heidi off her feet and into his arms. She pushed, struggling, but he leaned in and whispered low as he marched with firm, deliberate strides to his doorway.

"You will do what I say, and you will do what I say *now*. Stop causing a scene. We will get your sister. You are not going to that club. You will come with me to my apartment and act reasonably. You will stop acting like a child, before I treat you like one. Am I clear?"

She looked at him, her eyes wide and tear-filled. She nodded. "But my sister," she said, her voice catching. He could hear the fight going out of her as he reached his apartment and opened the door.

"Your sister will be fine, baby," he crooned. "We'll do every-thing we can." He walked over to the couch and gently released her. She curled up into a corner, as Paul came into the apartment and shut and locked the door behind him. Dom skewered her with a look. "Do. Not. Move." She looked at her hands, swallowed, and nodded.

Dom went to his entryway, took the bag from Paul, and thanked him with a nod.

"She ever lose her shit like this before?" Dom whispered, too low for her to hear.

"Never seen her do this," Paul responded in a whisper. "She's tight with her sister, though, and scared shitless. God, I'm glad you got her under control. I was about ready to take her in hand myself."

Dom chuckled. He liked this guy.

Paul's voice dropped even lower. "What are we going to do about this?"

"I'll tell you," Dom said. "But let's make sure Heidi knows everything that's going on."

He returned to the living room, where Heidi was rocking back and forth. She'd responded to his commands, and now he needed to reassure her. He bent and scooped her back into his arms.

"Stop picking me up like I'm a sack of potatoes," she muttered irritably. He momentarily ignored the rudeness, sat back on the couch, and nestled her in his lap. He looked at Paul.

"Do me a favor? Grab a few bottles of water from the fridge." Paul nodded.

The minute Paul stepped out of the room, Dom leaned over, fisted her hair firmly but gently, and tipped her head back, leaning in to whisper.

"You listen, and you listen well, little girl," he said sternly. He felt her grow still. "You've already earned yourself a spanking for that display out there. I know you're worried about your sister, and I get that. Believe me, I do, and this is going to work out. But there's never been a more important time for you to obey me. I need you to trust me. Now, unless you want to earn yourself a much harder spanking than I'm already planning on giving you, you'll do what you're told and drop the attitude. Am I clear?"

Her eyes met his, and she was searching, hoping. He knew she found what she was looking for when she nodded, her whispered, "Yes, sir. I'm sorry, Dom. I'm just so scared," catching on the last word.

He put a single finger under her chin. "I know, baby. But acting recklessly isn't going to help your sister. Do you understand me?"

"Yes, sir," she said again, as Paul entered the room with the waters. He could see his words had both chastened and reassured her.

"Good girl," Dom murmured. He took a bottle of water from Paul, opened it, and offered it to Heidi. She took a few long pulls from the bottle, and when she was done, she sighed.

He settled her on his lap, as Paul leaned against Dom's desk. Dom began.

"I've called my brother. He has an in with Black Box, and is on his way over there now. No doubt, this guy secured a private room, but I know my brother, and he won't stop until he's found her."

Heidi sighed. "Thank God," she said.

"Show me the messages," he said. She wordlessly handed him the phone. As he read over the emails, he could see why she'd been so panicked.

Do you like the idea of being powerless, Hillary? Tonight, I plan on showing you how erotic that can be. You'll be my slave, from the minute you set foot into the club until I give you leave. Everything of yours belongs to me, from your sweet tits to your sweet pussy. I'll cuff you when you enter the club, and you are not to raise your eyes or talk to anyone unless I give you permission. Once you enter, my word is law. Your entering nulls any safeword. Arrive on time, or we'll begin with a caning that will make sitting for the evening an impossibility.

"Shit," Dom muttered.

"It gets worse," Paul said. "You familiar with rape fantasy, Dom?"

Dom's stomach tightened. "Yeah," he said reluctantly.

Heidi tucked her head into Dom's chest. "I can't. I can't even think about it!" she said.

"Don't, baby," he said.

"Is there any way for her to escape? Can she get out?"

Dom sighed. "I'm not very familiar with their club by-laws, but I can tell you this, his forbidding safewording already puts him on rocky ground consensually. How is she supposed to tell him what she likes and what she doesn't? She's new to this, you say?"

Heidi nodded. "When I first read the messages, I thought maybe it was possible she had been into this for a while and I didn't know it. But, the emails only go back a month or so, so she couldn't have been into it for very long."

Dom swore. He wanted to go in himself, get that Marauder asshole and teach him a lesson. The mere idea of an innocent girl being taken into that place, forbidden to safeword, and used... the adrenaline surged through him, as his phone rang. Matteo.

"Yeah?" he asked. He put his finger to his lips to indicate Heidi was to remain quiet. She sat back meekly, but was clearly on alert.

"I'm here," Matteo said. "Slay's here and I've filled him in. We've got the owner notified, and he's joining us now. Thank God after that legal fiasco, he's not having any illegal activity."

"Good," Dom said. "You know what room she's in?"

"That's what we're trying to locate now," he said. "There are two dozen private rooms, and most are occupied tonight. Some shit convention or something."

"Dammit." Heidi's eyes widened, but he shook his head. "I'm

putting you on speaker, Matt." He pushed the button. "Matteo, Heidi's here, and Paul, her assistant."

"Hi, guys. I'm here with Slay, my friend the bouncer, and Mr. Gentry, the owner. Problem, Dom. There's no 'Marauder' on file. We need more information. No reservations last night from Marauder."

Paul looked thoughtful. "We could check her email for more information," he murmured. "There might even be a time-stamped message that would—" he froze, as if something clicked in his mind, then he shook his head as if to dismiss the idea. "In any event, the room wasn't reserved for tonight," Paul said. "It was *last* night. Whoever's got her, if he's still there, is going on day two."

"That narrows it down," Matteo replied. In the background, they could hear a woman's low scream, and Heidi gasped. "That's someone else, Heidi," Matteo said. "It's all good. That was a good scream."

Another voice came on. "Heidi? What does your sister look like? Give height and weight estimations, and any identifying marks. All women were masked when they entered, and several were hooded."

She closed her eyes, but when they opened she was determined. "She's about 5'4", about 130 pounds."

"Could be anyone. Dammit."

"Oh! She has two matching star tattoos she got on spring break last year. One under her left ear and the other on her right wrist." Muffled voices on the other end of the line, low swearing, then Matteo's voice.

"I'm gonna hang-up for now. That was a good clue, there, Heidi. Slay saw only one girl enter with tattoos that match that description, but we think she's been taken to the Sanctuary. We can't get in there easily. I'll fill you in later. But I need to be on my game. I'm hanging up now."

"Thanks, man," Dom said. Heidi was crying quietly.

"All right. I'll call you as soon as I have any news. Heidi, hang in there, honey." They could hear him running, and muffled voices before his phone clicked.

Heidi's head fell against Dom's chest as the phone disconnected.

"I know about the Sanctuary," Paul said quietly. Dom and Heidi both looked to him. "I knew a Master who used it for training purposes a few years back." Heidi winced. "It's a private suite traveling masters are allowed to rent for their slaves. It was above all other rooms, and extremely expensive because of the privacy and location. It's sound-proof."

The sat in silence for a few minutes, Heidi's shuddering breaths setting Dom on edge. He smoothed her hair with his hand and rubbed her shoulders. Paul looked awkwardly at the two of them.

"Glad to see you're being a good girl, now, Heids," Paul murmured. He smirked at her and gave Dom a knowing look. "That was some very *interesting* behavior there, wouldn't you say, *Dom?*"

Dom heard the emphasis on his name, and stifled a chuckle. He knew exactly what Paul was doing, and he was grateful for the attempt at lightening the situation.

"Shut. *Up,*" Heidi hissed at Paul. Paul raised his eyebrows. His eyes went to Dom.

"You let her speak to people that way?" his lips pressed together in an attempt not to grin.

Dom shook his head from side to side. "She gets naughtier and naughtier by the minute. I might need to do something about that."

Her eyes widened and mouth dropped open. "You *guys*!"

Dom chuckled, but as he did, his phone buzzed. They all stilled.

Found her in the Sanctuary. Bastard did her over bad, but she's safe. I've got her now. He got away. I've got her in the office, medics are arriving. She's okay.

Dom put his phone out of Heidi's reach. He didn't want her to see.

"They've got her. Matteo has her, and she's safe now."

She put her head on his chest and burst into tears.

Heidi lay next to him, running her fingers through the curly tufts of hair on his bare chest, a delicate fingernail tracing his hardened abs. "I'm sorry," she whispered.

"Shhh," he said, running his fingers through her hair. "I know you were overwhelmed. I know why you behaved that way. Over time, you'll learn to trust me more and it will become habitual to obey me."

Matteo had called, assured Dom that Hillary was okay, and said that she'd fallen asleep, crashing after the events of the night. He'd suggested it would be best for Heidi to wait to see her until the morning. Heidi had called her mom, and assured her Hillary was safe. Her mother had insisted she wanted to see her daughter, and gotten Heidi so near tears again, Dom had taken the phone from her and spoken to her mother himself.

"This is Heidi's boyfriend, Dom," he'd said. "I understand your concern, but Heidi's had a long and trying evening and needs to get some rest now. In the morning, we can all see Hillary. She's in good hands."

Her mother had been livid. "Dom! Dom who? I don't know you! Put my daughter back on the phone!"

"I can't do that," he'd insisted, his voice taking on the stern headmaster's immovable tone. "As I said, she needs rest and you'll see her in the morning."

"And how do I know Hillary is okay?"

"It was my brother who got her out," he'd said. "I know

you've had a trying night yourself, but I'm going to ask you one final time to please let Heidi rest, and trust me that Hillary is safe and resting herself."

She'd sighed. "Your brother rescued her?"

"Yes, ma'am."

And after a bit more persuasion, she'd agreed to his terms.

He'd given her no alternative.

They'd ordered pizza with Paul, who finally gave her a good-night hug as the wee hours of morning approached. "I'll check in on you in the morning, sweetie," he'd said. He'd given Dom a firm handshake. As the door shut behind him, Heidi had turned to Dom.

"Thank you," she'd whispered, putting her arms around his neck and squeezing. He'd lifted her, arms under her legs, carrying her to the bedroom. And now, as she lay with him, she was beginning to relax. Suddenly, she sat up.

"Princess!"

"I fed her, and took her out, and told her if she behaved I'd get her those gross bacon things," he said, pushing out of bed.

"You did?" she asked, her eyes softening. He turned, leaning back against his dresser.

"Yep."

"Oh! I need some clean clothes," she said. "I haven't done laundry this week, and—"

"Done," he said, gesturing to the bag he'd instructed Paul to leave by the door. Her eyes traveled to the bag, as if seeing it for the first time. "But you won't need anything to wear until the morning." She flushed and her eyes went to her hands. Her voice dropped.

"Am I… are you going to spank me?" she asked. He pursed his lips and crossed his arms.

"Mmm-hmmm," he stated.

She sighed. "I was kinda awful," she whispered.

"You weren't awful," he said kindly. "But you know you need

a spanking for behaving that way." She nodded, as he continued. "But you're very tired and should get some rest now. We can deal with this in morning."

She twisted her hands in her lap and bit her lip. "Please… sir?" she asked quietly. He nodded. "Could we get it over with? I feel…" she twisted her hand into a knot and tapped it up against her chest. "All—like this—inside," she whispered, her voice catching and her eyes filling with tears. "And… I want it over with."

He thought for a minute. Poor girl. She'd had a trying evening, between dealing with her mother, and worrying about her sister. She was right. She *did* need a spanking, and he knew that consistency, the relief of having her punishment over, and the stress relief the rush of being spanked would give her, would help. He wouldn't allow her to control this, but a meek request was certainly allowed. He nodded slowly.

"I understand," he said. He pushed himself off the dresser, and moved to the edge of the bed. He rolled up his sleeves, as he turned sideways to address her. "Go get out of your clothes and into one of my t-shirts," he said. "Then come to me and bring your hairbrush." She blinked, but nodded and stood, and it pleased him to see her obeying his instructions. When she returned to him, dressed in one of his t-shirts that just hit the top of her thighs, with the brush in hand, he patted his lap. "Come here and lie over my lap," he murmured. She took a deep breath and obeyed. He positioned her over his lap.

His tone was gentle, his touch firm but sensual, as he raised the edge of his t-shirt and bared her. "Why are you getting a spanking, little girl?" he asked in a husky voice. He could feel it already, the desire for her. Despite his exhaustion, despite the fact he was administering punishment, the desire to take her and claim her was as instinctive and natural as his desire to breathe.

"I was rude to you," she whispered. "I told you no, and yelled at Paul, and tried to disobey you, and didn't do what you told me to."

"That's right," he said, his voice just above a whisper, as he ran his hand down the smooth curve of her bare skin. "And why is it important to obey me?"

"Because you look out for me," she whispered, and her voice caught. "Because you… want what's best for me," she said.

"Yes, baby," he said. "I'm going to spank you now, Heidi, and I want you count with each stroke."

"Yes, sir," she said. He raised the brush and brought it down with a solid crack. She winced, but didn't cry out.

"One, sir."

He brought it down again, and again, and when she choked out a whispered, "Twenty," he dropped the brush to the bed and massaged her reddened skin.

"Keep counting," he commanded evenly, and after he rubbed the sting out, he raised his hand and brought it down again, feeling the sting on his own hand as he gave her a hard swat.

"Twenty-one, sir," she whispered, and that's when her tears began.

"Let it out," he directed, raising his hand and bringing it down again, "And no need to count anymore, baby." The tears flowed as his hand raised and came down again, softer, but with enough sting that the breath hissed out of her. He could her the soft catch of her cries, as he spanked her, but he knew she needed this, he knew she needed *him*, and that his taking control this way would bring her relief, comfort, and reassurance.

"You're a good girl, Heidi," he said, delivering another stinging slap, "and you try so hard. So hard." He knew she was done when she lay over his lap as limp as a rag doll. He lifted her up and she slid to the floor between his legs, her head on his knee, as he picked up the brush and ran it through her hair again. "Such a good girl," he murmured. When she looked so calm she looked as if she were asleep, he raised her chin.

"Feeling better, honey?" he asked.

"Yes," she said. He could see the relief written in her features, the weariness taking over now. He placed a tentative finger on her chest.

"That gone?" he asked. "That knot?"

"All gone," she whispered.

"Good girl," he said. "Now come up to bed." She crept up onto the bed and he pulled the blanket up around her. "I'm going to get ready for bed myself, now," he said. "I'll be back in a minute." And two minutes later, when he came back to her, she was already dead asleep. He watched her quietly for a minute. It pleased him to know he'd helped her relax, and gotten them back to where they needed to be—him in charge, her under his obedience, both content, and ready to put the night's events to rest.

—————

Dom drummed his fingers across the gleaming surface of his desk as his phone buzzed. He picked it up automatically, ready to respond if it was Heidi needing him. Although he'd left her safely tucked away at her apartment with her sister, a platter of brownies, and a pile of chick flicks, he still worried.

Hey. Just checking in. Everything okay?

He nodded at the dark corner of his office, and glanced out the large window just in time to see Jay's car pull in next to his in the parking lot. Everything was perfect.

Yep. All in place, ready to go. Will update. You good, babe?

It took a few seconds for her response to come, and he could picture the scene—Heidi sitting on the couch as she always did, one leg tucked under her, phone in her hand.

We're great. Just about to start 'The Notebook', bowl of popcorn at the ready. Just miss my man.

He smiled to himself.

I'll be back as soon as we're done here. Hang tight and be good.

I'm always good.

The hell she was. He dropped his phone back on the desk with a smirk when a knock came at the door.

"Come in," he said, using his deepest, most authoritative headmaster voice.

All Jay knew was that he'd been summoned to the headmaster's office on a Saturday. Dom hoped to hell he'd been sweating it out ever since he'd gotten the call.

Dom strategically folded his hands on his desk as the door swung open. Jay entered, his eyes wide and innocent-looking.

Bastard.

After the incident with Hillary, Paul hadn't hesitated in sharing the 'evidence' he'd discovered during the financial audit —money transferred in *Dom's* name, on *his* laptop, meant to incriminate him in the scandal that had almost brought the school to ruin. Dom had denied it, and they'd quickly found proof that Dom couldn't have made the transfer—he'd been checked into the gym with Heidi at the time, and they had the gym record to prove it. It had been easy enough to put two and two together after that. Jay had access, he had the opportunity, and he'd been seen in Dom's office.

Did Jay think he was stupid?

Dom held the record in front of him, the printout from the gym with the dated stamp on it.

"How are things, Jay?" he asked smoothly.

Jay merely nodded, and stood with his hands in his pockets.

"What gives, Dom?" he blustered. "Why'd you call me in here on a Saturday?"

"Sit down."

Jay blinked, as if deciding on whether or not to push the issue, before he shrugged and obeyed, folding himself into the chair opposite Dom.

"I think you know why."

Dom had already decided on his approach before he came.

He would be straightforward, cut to the chase, but give Jay just enough rope to hang himself.

Jay folded his arms across his chest, as his arrogant facade wore off and his eyes took on a hard edge. "I don't. Why don't you tell me?"

Dom coolly placed the papers he held in front of Jay.

"You know what these are?" he asked evenly.

"Nope."

"The first, is a transfer into the alumni donation account, requested in my name. Odd, considering you know I didn't make that transfer, and it was a large enough sum to cause our consultants to easily point out a major discrepancy."

Jay shook his head. "Tsk tsk."

The gall! Dom wanted to grab him by his scrawny neck and —he paused, and took a deep, cleansing breath. It wouldn't do to lose his shit now.

He pointed to the second paper. "And this, a time-stamped record of my arrival at my gym, corresponding exactly at the time I supposedly had my ass in this chair making the transfer."

Jay shrugged. "Your point?"

Dom narrowed his eyes and whispered, "You know you were the one responsible for that transfer. You were in here that afternoon when I came to retrieve Heidi's thumb drive—both of us saw you. I can't believe you had the nerve to use *my* name and incriminate *me* in this!"

Jay shook his head, but Dom persisted, knowing it was only a matter of time before he got what he needed.

"Your father would be *appalled*," he said. "Such a way to shame the Divris name."

That hit where it hurt. Jay's cheeks flushed.

"You'll never prove it!" he hissed.

"Prove what?" Dom asked low.

"You know *what*! That I transferred the money. And even if

you do try to bring that stupid paper in, my father will hear about this, and—"

Dom turned to the corner of the room and nodded.

"You got enough?"

Jay jumped to his feet, his eyes bulging, as Paul stepped out of the shadow.

"Got every word," he said smoothly, piercing Jay with a look. He handed the phone to Dom, and Dom nodded.

"Thanks, Paul. Time to make some phone calls."

Chapter 15

Heidi pushed the strap of her sundress back up her shoulder for the umpteenth time and looked at herself critically in the ornately gilded restroom mirror. Familiar grayish-blue eyes stared out from a face gone way too freckled in the summer sun, unremarkable brown hair waved down her back, maybe a little longer than she'd usually wore it, since Dom liked it a bit longer. But all in all, not a single outward change from the woman she'd been four months ago. Inside, though...

Heidi gave the woman in the mirror a secret smile.

The door to the lobby opened, letting in a burst of loud chatter from the restaurant beyond. Though *Cara*, Tony's restaurant, was normally closed on a Sunday afternoon, he'd made an exception for today's private party.

"If you don't get out here in the next five minutes, our mother is going to run off with your boyfriend," Hillary joked, approaching the mirror.

Heidi's smile deepened and she grabbed the lipstick from her purse.

"Paul assured me that the whole new-romance, staring-into-space thing would pass once Dom and I hit the four-month mark, but it's still going strong," Heidi confessed, leaning forward to apply the color to her mouth.

"Four months is the standard, huh?" Hillary asked, one eyebrow raised. "No way to cut it shorter than that?"

"Not according to *Paul*," Heidi said. "He says it takes this long for things to calm down and settle into a rhythm."

She leaned forward and wiped a stray bit of color from the edge of her mouth before continuing.

"I'm sure it works that way for some people, but Dom's a force of nature, you know?" She met Hillary's eyes in the mirror and smiled. "There's a *lot* to process. I was just standing here wondering how I could possibly look so normal on the outside, when everything's been blown to bits and put back together on the inside." She shook her head. "It's hard to explain."

"I get it," Hillary said slowly, coming up behind Heidi and smoothing Heidi's hair the way she had when they were kids. "It's like... like someone took all the pieces that make you *you* and didn't—*change them*, exactly, just—took them apart and put them back together with stronger glue, with a firm foundation. Like you're more solidly yourself when you're with him."

Heidi spun around, startled.

"That's *exactly* it. Hillie, how did you know?"

Hillary blushed and studied the floor. "Oh, um... Well, I don't actually *know* what it feels like. I mean, how *could* I, right? I guess I just... read a lot. You know?"

But the note of pain in her stammered reply made Heidi's heart twist in sympathy.

"Honey," she said, reaching out to push Hillie's hair back from her face. "I can't even imagine what you went through last spring..."

Hillary hadn't wanted to give more than the most basic details about her ordeal at Black Box, and Heidi, with encouragement from Dom, had opted not to push. She'd let Hillary tell her when she was ready. Still…

"I hope you know you can talk to me about it, if you want to. And I hope it hasn't made you give up on the idea of romance completely. Your Prince Charming is out there somewhere, I'm sure of it."

Hillary shook her head, then smirked. "Are we really doing this? *You* are telling *me* to hold out for true love? Things really *have* changed," she teased.

Heidi smacked her lightly on the arm.

"Yeah, well, falling in love is like that," she said, turning back to the mirror to pull up the strap of her sundress once again. "You suddenly see hearts and rainbows everywhere, and you want everyone to be as happy as you are."

"Oooh, so you guys are finally using the l-word?" Hillary asked, her eyes wide. "That's awesome!"

"Well… we haven't said it out loud, not officially," Heidi admitted. "But… I know he loves me, and he knows the same."

She could hear the note of defensiveness in her own voice and grimaced. Why *hadn't* they said that to one another yet? It seemed like the kind of thing Dom should initiate, but then… Maybe he was waiting for her to do it. As much as Dom was in control of their relationship, he was always careful to avoid rushing her or pushing too hard.

"*Honestly*?" Hillary said derisively. "Heidi, you know he loves you. You know that he has your back. You know that he's your rock, your anchor. *Show him that you know that.* Show him that *you know* you don't need to be afraid of that stuff any more. You're lucky enough to have found the man you love *and* to know that he loves you *back*! Don't waste time, Heids."

Heidi frowned. It sounded like Hillary was speaking from experience.

"Hillie, please talk to me," she implored. "I want to help you."

But Hillary would not be sidetracked.

"I know you do. But there's only one thing you can do to help me: tell him you love him. Be brave." Hillary gave her a half-smile. "Set a good example for me, big sister. Remind me that dreams do come true."

Heidi nodded and wrapped her arms around Hillary, wishing she could somehow turn back time and erase everything that had dimmed the spark of joy that had always lit her sister's eyes. The past few months had fundamentally changed Hillary, making her more mature, more introspective, and more subdued.

Hillary eased back from the hug and gave Heidi a wink.

"Now, get out there before Mom convinces Dom that he's always had a burning desire to take up naked bongo drumming on a commune in Ohio, okay?"

Heidi laughed. Their mother's first 'meeting' with Dom over the phone had been discouraging to say the least. She'd called her mother the next morning with her heart in her throat, ready to defend Dom's defense of *her*... only to have her mother gush about how 'wonderful' Dom had been to take charge of things the way he had, and how 'relieved' she was that Heidi had found a guy who 'championed' her needs that way.

"Baby," Dom had told her smugly, when she'd relayed the conversation to him. "I think your mother's needed a firm hand for the past two decades!"

Not an idea I want to entertain, Heidi thought wryly as she stepped from the dimly lit bathroom into the sun-splashed lobby. But the way her mother gushed over Dom and hung on his every word seemed to indicate that he was right.

She put the thought out of her mind as she nodded hello to Tessa, the friendly brunette Tony had hired as a manager and event coordinator just a couple of months ago, who was chatting with Paul's boyfriend, John, by the hostess desk.

"Hey, chickie," John greeted her, dropping a kiss on her cheek.

"Hey, you. Behaving yourself?" she asked with a wink.

"Always," he smirked, understanding the double meaning behind the innocent question in a way that others, like Tessa, couldn't. "Except when I don't."

Heidi laughed, all too familiar with that feeling.

Tessa snickered, too, before turning it into a cough… leading Heidi to question just how much the pretty manager actually *did* understand.

"Seriously, though," John said, as they nodded goodbye to Tessa and he steered Heidi through the empty restaurant to the private function room where their friends and families waited. "Things are going really well. Tessa just said that they're looking for a pastry chef, and Tony gave her my name. This place is about to explode in popularity thanks to Tessa, and if I could get in here… I think it would be good for both me *and* the restaurant. Paul says I'm the most talented pastry chef in Boston," he said proudly.

"Really?" Heidi teased as they ducked beneath a suffocating array of crepe-paper streamers to enter the room. "See, I heard Paul say you were talented, but I didn't think it was your *pastry* he was referring to…"

John's eyes widened in mock outrage, making Heidi laugh. "Oooh! You did *not* just say that! I'm telling Dom."

"Telling Dom what?" came a deep, gravelly voice in her ear, just as strong arms wrapped around her from behind.

Heidi leaned back, resting her head against Dom's shoulder, thrilling at his touch even as she glared at John. "Yeah, John," she challenged, "Telling Dom *what?*"

"Er…" John hesitated. "Telling Dom…um… *Congratulations!*" He smiled widely at Dom. "I mean, *of course!* It *is* your party, right?"

"You are the world's worst liar," Paul said severely, handing John a flute of champagne as he joined them. "I couldn't even hear what you were talking about and I can tell you were lying."

John sighed as he took a sip, and Heidi knew he was fighting an eye-roll that would have earned him a punishment... knew it, because she was fighting one herself.

"I was just congratulating Dom on his new job," John told Paul. "It's a huge opportunity! We're really happy for you," he told Dom.

Paul gave Dom a chin-lift. "He's right. We are. Easterbrook's loss is Association's gain. They're lucky to have you."

Heidi couldn't restrain herself. "Now that you don't suspect my boyfriend of embezzlement, you mean?" she joked.

She expected Paul's pursed lips and raised eyebrow, but even after all these months, she'd failed to anticipate Dom's not-quite-painful-but-decidedly-not-playful pinch at her waist, or his sternly whispered, "Heidi."

She cleared her throat.

"I was just kidding," she told Paul seriously. "Especially after everything you did to save the day!"

Paul looked slightly mollified, though she wasn't sure whether that was because of what she'd said or Dom's not-so-subtle rebuke.

"Wait, what? You went all superhero and didn't tell me?" John asked.

"Oh, gosh, that's right! You guys had just started dating when all of that went down," Heidi realized. And she recounted the story of the bribes, the lost income, the scholarship kids who'd have no way to pay tuition, and the way it appeared that Dom had been involved in the whole mess.

"So what did you do?" John asked Paul, his eyes wide.

Paul shrugged. "Well, as Heidi *mentioned*," he said, giving her a sharp glance that made her squirm, "I fell for it. At least at first. But then Heidi reminded me that there was another explanation."

Heidi nodded. "Turns out *Jay Divris* from the Finance Department had been getting kickbacks for admitting under-qualified applicants. And then once he learned that the Board of Directors had hired us to do a financial audit, he used Dom's computer to make some money transfers and update some files, to make it look like Dom was the one who'd been doing it. He even went around stealing copies of financial reports, trying to clean up his mess." This time, she didn't fight the eye roll.

"Geez! So, did you make him give back all the money?" John asked Paul.

Paul shook his head. "I wish we could have. Unfortunately, the police felt like there wasn't enough evidence to prosecute him."

Paul's expression showed exactly how he'd felt about that injustice.

"The best we could do," Dom interjected, "was fire his ass. Since the only reason he got the job in the first place was through his connections on the board, I know he'll find it pretty hard to find another position that will help him make the payments on his Lexus."

"But what about the kids?" John asked. "If he didn't pay back the money…"

Paul and Dom exchanged a knowing look and a smile. Heidi giggled.

"Well, it should come as no surprise that our guys are pretty tough negotiators," Heidi told John.

His eyes widened and he nodded.

"There wasn't enough evidence for a confession," Paul said. "But there was definitely enough to tarnish the Divris name. So, Dom and I went to Mr. Divris, *Senior*, otherwise known as the Head of the Board of Directors. He was happy to make a personal donation large enough to cover the shortfall, as long as we kept the story out of the media."

"Not to mention, he now gets a reputation as quite a philanthropist," Dom said dryly.

Heidi agreed. And she also privately felt that Mr. Divris,

whose family had attended Easterbrook for generations and who had been genuinely appalled at his son's behavior, had been moved to write the check for sentimental reasons—for the good of the school.

"Well, no wonder you decided to move on!" John told Dom. "Get away from the drama."

Dom shrugged. "I never liked dealing with the board, so I won't miss that BS. But I'll miss the kids."

Heidi squeezed his hands where they rested at her waist and felt him squeeze her in return. She knew the decision to leave Easterbrook for his new role as Head of Financial Aid for the New England Association of Private Schools had been a difficult one for him. Helping kids was the whole reason he'd been drawn to education in the first place. But as she'd gently reminded him, now he'd be in a position to help even more deserving kids obtain scholarships and help them succeed.

"Congratulations, brother," Matteo said as he joined their group, batting aside more of the crepe paper that hung like Spanish moss from the ceiling so he could clap Dom on the shoulder. "Happy for you."

He nodded a greeting at Paul and John, then ducked his head to give Heidi a kiss on the cheek, handing her a flute of champagne.

"Looking pretty as a picture today, Heids," he told her. Then he glanced pointedly at her shoulder, where her stupid strap had fallen down again.

She tugged it back into place and shook her head. Matteo was a pain in the ass, but he was a lovable one.

"Thanks, Matt," she said. "I'm so glad you could come."

"Wouldn't miss it," he said sincerely. "But honey, could you have toned down these decorations?" He swiped at the multicolored paper and ribbons hanging from the ceiling. "Trees gave their lives for these things," he teased.

Heidi smothered a laugh.

"Don't look at me! My contributions to this party were the 'Congratulations!' banner and the cake from the bakery," she said with a smile, sipping her champagne as she leaned her head against Dom's throat. "Tony coordinated everything."

"Tony did this?" Matteo looked around, bewildered. "Where did we go wrong with him, Dom? We're going to have to stage an intervention."

John snickered.

"Hush! It wasn't his idea. It was Val's," Heidi told them in a low voice. "She told Tony it 'needed pizazz,' and she ran to Party Plaza."

"Jesus," Dom said. She could feel him shaking his head. "And I bet she got his credit card first."

"You can imagine how she felt about Tessa's ideas for redecorating this place next month," John interjected. "Tessa is going for classic, clean lines—that's what draws a high-end clientele these days. But *Val* said it needs more color, and she's harping on Tony to bring in some interior designer she knows. Tessa's too professional to say so, but I'm pretty sure she's ready to commit murder."

Matteo shot Dom a worried glance.

"We really *might* need to stage an intervention," he said, and Heidi could feel Dom nod.

Then Hillary walked into the room, brushing aside streamers with an annoyed frown, and all of them stopped talking to watch her. She started towards Heidi and Dom, a smile on her face, then seemed to notice the other members of their group and stopped short. She gave a little wave, abruptly turned and walked in the opposite direction. Heidi frowned.

"How's she doing?" Paul asked, a thread of concern in his voice.

"I don't know," Heidi admitted. "Most of the time, she seems to be fine, but then…" Heidi blew out a breath. "I think graduating from college and moving down here is going to be good for her, but it'll be a big adjustment for her, too. I'm worried that she'll have a hard time finding a job. I'm worried that she'll have trouble with guys…" She shook her head, then turned to look at Matteo. "You know, Matt, I've actually been meaning to ask you —could *you* keep an eye on her, maybe?"

Dom stiffened behind her, and Matteo's eyes widened with uncharacteristic dread.

"Uh… *me*? You know, Heidi, honey, I don't think I'm really the best one to—"

"Please," she begged. "I know Hillie likes you, *trusts* you. You helped her so much in the days after… well, after what happened last spring. And I think it would be easier for her to have someone around who *wasn't* her big sister… or like a big brother," she added, squeezing Dom's arm. "Someone who could just be a friend, you know?"

Matteo looked at Dom helplessly and swallowed hard. "Well, I… yeah, I guess I could do that. I could keep an eye on her."

"In a *friendly sort of way*," Dom reminded him.

"Right, exactly. Obviously," Matteo agreed.

"Thanks, Matt," she said, stepping away from Dom and standing on tiptoe to press a kiss to Matteo's cheek.

"Uh… sure," he said. "No problem." Then, turning quickly to John and Paul, he asked, "Can I buy you gents a drink?"

As the others wandered off to the bar, Heidi turned to face Dom and wrapped her arm around his waist while she took another sip of champagne.

"I feel like I've hardly seen you today," she commented.

"Mmm," he agreed. He lifted a hand to pull up the strap of her dress which had fallen once more. "Showing a lot of skin there, baby."

Heidi pressed her lips together to bite back a retort that might earn her a swat.

"Yes. Because these dress straps don't stay up. Which is what I told you this morning, when you picked out this dress, sir," she reminded him sweetly.

He wrapped both his hands around her waist, and his eyes sparkled. "Hmmm... I think I do remember you telling me that."

Heidi smiled. Adorable, infuriating man.

"So, if you heard me tell you that, why did you have me wear it?" she asked.

"Maybe," he said, leaning down to nuzzle her neck, "because I like when you show a little skin."

Heidi shivered. She would never get used to this man, never take this magic for granted. Hillary's words from earlier came back to her. It was time to tell him...

"Dom..." she began hesitantly. "I need to tell you, I—"

At the last moment, her resolve failed her—she couldn't force the words past a lump in her throat. She nervously threw back the rest of her drink, gathering her courage.

Dom frowned.

"That's enough champagne," he warned her.

"Yes, okay," she agreed easily. "It's just... I want to say that..."

"I'm not kidding," he interrupted, grabbing the glass from her hand and setting it on a nearby table with a click. "No more drinking today, Heidi."

She inhaled deeply and gathered her patience. He was ruining her perfect moment!

"Another rule?" she asked crossly.

His eyes narrowed at her tone. "Yeah," he confirmed. "Another rule. Problem?"

Heidi blew out a breath.

"No," she said. Then, seeing his raised eyebrow, grudgingly added, "Sir."

Dom eyed her speculatively for a moment, and a knot formed in Heidi's stomach—a combination of anxiety and anticipation. She was being disrespectful and she knew better, but he wouldn't punish her here, would he? With all of their friends and family around? The knot in her belly grew tighter as she realized that he definitely *would*. And the rest of the restaurant was empty…

"So, Hillie's moving to Boston in a few weeks," he said, the abrupt change of subject jolting her from her thoughts.

Shoot. Was he waiting so that he could punish her more thoroughly back at home later? If so, that would make it doubly bad —the anticipation would kill her. But she couldn't *ask* without inviting more punishment and he *knew* it. His eyes fairly sparkled. *Drat.*

She was so distracted she almost neglected to reply—and that would've bought her even more trouble, for not listening.

"Uh… Two weeks from tomorrow. Right," Heidi confirmed. "She's going to be staying on my sofa, like we talked about. Now that you and Paul have finally gotten me to buy furniture for the place." She added the last in a teasing tone, inviting him to smile.

It didn't work.

"She needs a place of her own," he told her firmly.

Heidi stepped back to look at him, her surprise no doubt reflected on her face.

"But… Dom, how can she afford it? She doesn't have a—"

"Are you arguing with me, little girl?" he asked.

Crap.

"No, sir," she whispered. "I'm just… um… expressing a concern. She doesn't have a job and—"

"I'm aware of that, Heidi. Which is why I think she should live at *your* place," he said, his eyes sparkling.

"I… Okay, I'm confused," Heidi admitted. "Isn't that what I just said?"

Dom laughed. "Hillary can live at your place, and *you* can move in with *me.*"

"Y-you… and I?" Heidi stammered, a spark of hope igniting in her chest.

It was the first step in a future she'd been thinking about

practically since their first meeting—moving in together, getting married, having a family—seeing how their relationship would change and grow at each stage of the journey, how they'd work together to make it beautiful. Still, the idea of it happening, of it starting *right now* took her breath away.

"You're there practically every night anyway," he reminded her.

"Well, yes, that's true…"

"Princess's bowl is in my kitchen, and my key is on your key ring," he added.

"I know, you're right, it's just…"

"Just what, baby?"

"It's just… I didn't think you'd want to do it so soon! We've only been together four months!"

"So?"

"So! So—that's—only *four months!*"

He shrugged. "Four months is long enough when you love someone."

He said it as if it were a simple statement of fact, a given.

"When you… love someone?" she repeated. She felt tears come to her eyes, and her face softened as he looked at her.

He led her to the furthest corner of the room, a darkened alcove mercifully free of decoration, and pushed her gently back against the wall, bracing a hand above her head so that his body blocked her view of the room.

"Heidi," he said, lifting his free hand to stroke his thumb over her cheek. "Why do I give you all those rules, baby?"

Heidi glanced up at him, and his tender expression nearly brought her to her knees.

Why did he give her rules? So many reasons, and they all swam in her head. He liked being in control, that was the simplest answer—the smartass answer she'd have given him when they first met. But now she knew that was only the smallest part of his motivation. He was a dominant because he had a need to protect—he gave her rules because he wanted to keep her safe. And, she admitted to herself, he had known, even before she was ready to admit it, that she *liked* giving him control, *needed* to give him control... and he met that need for her.

"Because..." she licked her dry lips. "Because you... want to take care of me and keep me safe, and because you know I need those rules."

He nodded, his fingers playing with the hair at her temple.

"I've never wanted to do that for anyone before," he said. "Not this way. I never felt the need to protect someone, to take care of someone, the way I do for you. I love you."

Heidi's breath caught in her throat and a rush of emotion that threatened to overwhelm her. Happiness, possessiveness, relief, joy, protective tenderness, unbreakable connection... She'd once thought those emotions were for other people, until Dom. This man made her feel so much!

"And why do you follow the rules, Heidi? Why don't you tell me to back off? Why do you put your phone away before you drive? Baby, why are you wearing *this dress*?"

Heidi took a deep breath and found that she didn't need champagne courage, or a perfect moment, she just needed to trust Dom. And she did, in every part of her. She always had.

She slid her hands up around his neck and looked directly into his eyes.

"Because I love you, too," she said. Her voice was low, but she spoke the words clearly and confidently. They *were* a statement of fact. It *was* a given.

Still, she could tell by the fire in his eyes that Dom had needed to hear it.

"Yeah," he said softly. "You do."

Heidi burst out laughing, her arms tightening around his neck as he leaned down to brush his lips gently over hers.

"Later," he promised her, when she would have deepened the kiss.

He stepped back, smiled at her, then oh-so-slowly slid the strap of her dress back into place once again.

She felt her nipples tighten at the caress, and knew by his smirk that it was one hundred percent intentional. He knew exactly what he was doing to her.

Her eyes narrowed. Submissive she might be, but two could play at this game.

As Dom wrapped an arm around her waist and led her back to the party, Heidi signaled to one of the many waiters circulating with trays of drinks and hors d'oeuvres, who immediately approached and offered her a glass of champagne.

"Thank you," Heidi told the waiter with a bright smile, accepting the glass.

The waiter nodded and moved on, but Dom had frozen solid beside her.

"Was I not clear about the rule?" he asked, his voice deceptively casual while his eyes surveyed the room.

"The rule?" Heidi pursed her lips and pretended to think about it. "Oh! The brand new no-more-drinking rule!"

"That's the one," he said, turning his head to look at her. "And I warn you, little girl, that was no joke."

It just wasn't fair the way his stern voice *did things* to her belly!

"No joke?" she asked, infusing her voice with just the right amount of innocent disappointment. "So, you're saying that if I take even one *teeny*, tiny sip of this champagne," she swirled the bubbly liquid for effect, "you'll have to punish me?"

"I will," he said, and his tone left no doubt that he was serious… even as his eyes lit with excitement he couldn't contain.

"I understand, sir," she told him meekly.

Then she drained her glass.

The End

Jane Henry

USA Today bestselling author Jane Henry pens stern but loving alpha heroes, feisty heroines, and emotion-driven happily-ever-afters. She writes what she loves to read: kink with a tender touch. Jane is a hopeless romantic who lives on the East Coast with a houseful of children and her very own Prince Charming.

Don't miss these exciting titles by Jane Henry and Blushing Books!

A Thousand Yesses

Bound to You series
Begin Again, Book 1
Come Back To Me, Book 2
Complete Me, Book 3

Boston Doms Series
By Jane Henry and Maisy Archer
My Dom, Book 1
His Submissive, Book 2
Her Protector, Book 3
His Babygirl, Book 4
His Lady, Book 5
Her Hero, Book 6
My Redemption, Book 7

Anthologies

Hero Undercover
Sunstrokes

Connect with Jane Henry
janehenrywriter.blogspot.com
janehenrywriter@gmail.com

Maisy Archer

Maisy is an unabashed book nerd who has been in love with romance since reading her first Julie Garwood novel at the tender age of 12. After a decade as a technical writer, she finally made the leap into writing fiction several years ago and has never looked back. Like her other great loves - coffee, caramel, beach vacations, yoga pants, and her amazing family - her love of words has only continued to grow... in a manner inversely proportional to her love of exercise, house cleaning, and large social gatherings. She loves to hear from fellow romance lovers, and is always on the hunt for her next great read.

Don't miss these exciting titles by Jane Henry and Maisy Archer with Blushing Books!

Boston Doms Series
By Jane Henry and Maisy Archer
My Dom, Book 1
His Submissive, Book 2
Her Protector, Book 3
His Babygirl, Book 4
His Lady, Book 5
Her Hero, Book 6
My Redemption, Book 7

Anthologies
Hero Undercover
Sunstrokes

Connect with Maisy Archer
janeandmaisy.com

Blushing Books

Blushing Books is one of the oldest eBook publishers on the web. We've been running websites that publish spanking and BDSM related romance and erotica since 1999, and we have been selling eBooks since 2003. We hope you'll check out our hundreds of offerings at http://www.blushingbooks.com.

CPSIA information can be obtained
at www.ICGtesting.com
Printed in the USA
LVHW101704180723
752817LV00017B/81